***Alex Harrison was offering her
_____ as-marble
_____ sition.***

m correctly. She
tic blue eyes.

"Your wife?

He held up a hand. "My wife in name only.
Kate's nanny in fact. A simple business
arrangement that solves all short-term problems."
Alex reached out and touched Maggie's arm. "Is
it so terrible?" he asked.

An electric current passed between them at the
unexpected touch. Maggie was aware of a
quickening of her pulse.

For several long seconds they sat in silence. "If it
weren't for Kate, I'd walk away from this
ridiculous conversation."

"If it weren't for Kate, we wouldn't be having
this conversation at all." Alex stood.

She took a deep breath, met his eyes and held out
a hand to seal the deal.

"You've just bought yourself a wife. When's
our wedding?"

Dear Reader,

This July, Silhouette Romance cordially invites you to a month of marriage stories, based upon *your* favorite themes. There's no need to RSVP; just pick up a book, start reading…and be swept away by romance.

The month kicks off with our Fabulous Fathers title, *And Baby Makes Six,* by talented author Pamela Dalton. Two single parents marry for convenience' sake, only to be surprised to learn they're expecting a baby of their own!

In Natalie Patrick's *Three Kids and a Cowboy,* a woman agrees to stay married to her husband just until he adopts three adorable orphans, but soon finds herself longing to make the arrangement permanent. And the romance continues when a beautiful wedding consultant asks her sexy neighbor to pose as her fiancé in *Just Say I Do* by RITA Award-winning author Lauryn Chandler.

The reasons for weddings keep coming, with a warmly humorous story of amnesia in Vivian Leiber's *The Bewildered Wife;* a new take on the runaway bride theme in *Have Honeymoon, Need Husband* by Robin Wells; and a green card wedding from debut author Elizabeth Harbison in *A Groom for Maggie.*

Here's to your reading enjoyment!

Melissa Senate
Senior Editor
Silhouette Romance

Please address questions and book requests to:
Silhouette Reader Service
U.S.: 3010 Walden Ave., P.O. Box 1325, Buffalo, NY 14269
Canadian: P.O. Box 609, Fort Erie, Ont. L2A 5X3

A GROOM
FOR MAGGIE

Elizabeth Harbison

Silhouette
ROMANCE™
Published by Silhouette Books
America's Publisher of Contemporary Romance

To Barbara K. Atkins; I'm so glad you left your country to join our family.
Thanks to Natalie Patrick, Dani Sinclair and Jo-Ann Power for reading and advising. Special thanks to my sister Elaine Fox, and Marsha Nuccio aka M.L. Gamble, inspiring writers and wonderful friends.

 SILHOUETTE BOOKS

ISBN 0-373-19239-8

A GROOM FOR MAGGIE

Copyright © 1997 by Elizabeth Harbison

ELIZABETH HARBISON

first thought of becoming a writer in sixth grade, when she would stay up well past midnight reading Nancy Drew and Trixie Beldon books under the covers by flashlight. The idea became a decision when she discovered the books of Mary Stewart and Dorothy Eden, and realized that writing would be a really *fun* thing to do for a living.

She studied literature and art history at the University of Maryland and the University of London, Birbeck College. She's been back to England once since college and is eager to return again, and possibly even set a book there.

Also the author of several cookbooks, Elizabeth spends her spare time cooking, reading, walking and shopping for new books. As for romance, her fairy-tale dreams came true in 1994 when she married her real-life hero, John, a musician and illustrator. They currently reside in Germantown, Maryland, with their daughter, Mary Paige, and dog, Bailey.

Elizabeth loves to hear from readers. You can write to her c/o Silhouette Books, 300 E. 42nd Street, 6th floor, New York, NY 10017.

EIGHT WAYS TO GET
YOUR BOSS TO MARRY YOU
by nanny Maggie Weller

1) Remember to mix business and pleasure at *every* opportunity.

2) Men love a challenge–voice your opinion, even when you disagree with him (or *especially* when you disagree with him!).

3) Show him how to be the perfect dad to the daughter he has trouble relating to.

4) Love his daughter as if she were your own.

5) Let your work visa expire so you need to get married to stay in the U.S. (oops!)

6) Lock yourself in a wine cellar alone with him (it's the perfect way to *really* get close!).

7) If at first you don't succeed, try, try again.

8) When he offers you a marriage of convenience, show him how much better a marriage for real can be!

Chapter One

"Maggie, I don't know how else to say this. There was nothing I could do. You're going to have to leave the country next week."

"*Next week?*" Maggie Weller touched her fingers to her lips and sank slowly into the chair behind her.

"Next week. When my people were digging around to try to get an extension, they discovered that your visa expires even sooner than we thought. I have the information here."

"No." Maggie's eyes never left those of Alex Harrison, her employer and the father of her charge, five-year-old Kate. "That can't be," she said, feeling more an outsider than at any other point in the past year. For the first time, her own British accent sounded foreign even to her. "You're mistaken."

He concentrated on the papers in front of him. Was he avoiding her eyes? "It's all right here in black-and-white."

The cliché and his casual use of it hurt her. But of

course this was just a little business glitch for him. Sensitivity wasn't called for. Regardless of her feelings for him, to him she was just a commodity called "nanny."

She'd learned to ignore her feelings for him long ago. He would never see her as anything but an employee.

"Then *they've* obviously made a mistake," she said.

"I wish that were the case." For a moment he sounded as if he really meant it, but then he added two simple, yet dismissive words. "It's not."

Maggie wrung her hands in her lap. "I was very careful about timing when I signed up for my courses and committed to this position here with Kate. Even without the extension, I should have had at least six weeks before I had to go!"

He shook his head, his cool blue eyes sending a message Maggie couldn't read. Interest? Her heart pounded. Sympathy? Or was it anger that she had put him in a tight spot?

The paneled walls of his office closed in around her, and the leather-back chair suddenly felt hot and slick against her skin. Maggie had put too much faith in his ability to get her an extension. Somehow the possibility that she would have to leave had never seemed real. Now it seemed her departure was imminent. The house, young Kate, him... How would she ever say goodbye?

"You can see it for yourself." Alex passed her a document and their fingertips touched for a long moment when she took it. His eyes stayed on her.

It was Maggie who drew away first. She bit her lower lip, fighting the tingle that shot up her arm from his touch. In all the months she'd lived in this house with Alex Harrison, she'd been constantly on edge, as acutely aware of him as he'd seemed unaware of her.

For a second she sensed a change in his awareness, but only for a second.

Alex continued speaking as she read the paper. "I've already spoken with your embassy and my attorney. There's nothing that can be done." For a fraction of a second he hesitated, as if he were going to say something but changed his mind.

"I could immigrate," Maggie said without hope.

"My secretary checked into that. The waiting list is long. They are still working on applicants from…" He looked down at the papers on his desk.

"Nine years ago," Maggie finished dully. She looked at him, this time taking in everything, from the tailored DuBose suit, to the strong chiseled cheekbones and chin, and those unreadable eyes. A trace of dark beard shadowed his jaw and his gleaming dark hair was uncharacteristically ruffled, as though he'd been running his hand through it in that way he did when he was working on an important business deal.

"Nine years," she repeated. "I know. I've spoken with them myself. I just can't believe I could make this sort of error. My classes don't end for three weeks." She stopped, thinking of how close she was to receiving certification from the Maryland Montessori Institute. With that in hand she could get a good teaching job almost anywhere in the world.

Anywhere but the U.K., that is, where the unemployment rate in her village was astronomically high.

Most importantly, there was Kate Harrison to consider. How could Maggie leave Kate in the lurch? She'd spent countless hours studying the delicacy of the child's heart, and how best to nurture it. Abandonment was not part of the plan. "I promised Kate I'd be here for her birthday in July. I can't just disappear."

A muscle ticked in his jaw. "I'm sorry."

"She'll feel abandoned. It's not like she has that many people she can depend on." *And it's not as if you are going to be much comfort to her,* she wanted to add.

In the five months she had been working as a live-in nanny for Kate, she had debated with Alex Harrison more than once about his lack of personal attention to his daughter. If she hadn't known how coldhearted workaholics like him tended to be about family, she would have thought he was afraid to get close to his daughter.

But Maggie knew better. Work came above all else for him.

"What with her mother gone and you...so busy." The word tasted like a lie, even though she knew he believed it. "I can't do this to her. There *has* to be something I can do. Can't I apply for another extension?"

He shook his head. "You've already had one. It is virtually impossible to get a second, even though you're employed." He shrugged, letting her hopes drop like a lead ball. "I'll have to get Kate a new nanny. Again."

Maggie felt like he'd slapped her. He was reminding her of her place, whether he meant to or not. She was only an employee, hired to perform a function. For the thousandth time she realized Alex Harrison didn't see her as a woman. Or as human—with a heart. "Am I so easily replaced?"

His eyes clouded and Maggie instantly regretted the level of emotion in her voice. "Of course Kate will miss you," he said. "I was simply stating a fact. If you're leaving, I'll need to find a replacement."

"Of course." What was she hoping for? An eleventh hour claim of love from him? "But let me state a fact of my own. It's going to be very hard on Kate if we can't find a better solution.''

Alex sighed. ''Maggie, since her mother died a year ago, Kate has had six nannies, none of whom worked out for longer than four weeks. Two of them stole things from the house, one of them nipped at the bottle and three of them couldn't handle what they called Kate's 'temper tantrums'—''

''Cries for help,'' Maggie said, interrupting him. This was the side of Alex that she wasn't so crazy about— the side that refused to see the painful obviousness of his daughter's emotions. ''You can't expect a five-year-old not to be traumatized by her mother's death, and to act that trauma out. Then to be shipped off to live with a father she'd barely seen since a divorce when she was two…it must have been tremendously difficult for her.''

''I agree.'' Alex tried to keep his tone matter-of-fact, but he couldn't help the tremor of emotion that crept in. ''I hated seeing her go through that, and I hated feeling powerless to help. You are the seventh nanny this year and believe me, the fact that you've been here for five months has been a miracle. Kate's been doing great with you—I did everything in my power to keep you here.''

Maggie didn't seem to hear him, or at least the last part of what he said. ''It took more than a month for her to calm down to one outburst a day. Now she hasn't had one in months. My leaving and someone new coming in is going to undo all that progress.''

''Possibly. But there are no options.'' Alex shrugged, shutting away the powerful feelings of inadequacy his daughter's situation evoked in him. Feeling bad about it didn't do anybody any good. ''My people have looked into *all* the possibilities.''

"Then it will be up to you to get Kate through the transition," she challenged Alex. "I hope you realize that."

He tensed. How could he help Kate, when she was more afraid of him than anything else? Every time he was in a room with her, she became wary, with eyes darting for the door. When he spoke to her, she looked like a cornered rabbit.

He'd tried. Heaven knew, when he first got Kate back after her mother's death, he'd been wholly optimistic. He'd been happy for the chance to have his daughter back, close to him. But it hadn't taken long to see that Kate hadn't thought of him nearly as much as he'd thought of her. And she clearly didn't want to be in his house. She said it every night for three months: *I want to go home. I don't like you.*

Maggie wouldn't believe that, of course. She'd never understand. With her, Kate was the sweetest, gentlest child alive. Alex himself couldn't believe she was the same Kate who had come to him a year ago. Maybe it was men in general she was afraid of, or maybe it was him in particular, he didn't know. But if Maggie left, and it were up to him to be with Kate, there was no telling what sort of trauma she would experience.

And he didn't want to do it to her.

"Don't concern yourself with what happens after you go," he said, trying to prevent Maggie from driving the stake deeper into his heart.

"I'm very concerned. You have to start learning to be a father so that child has some *consistency* in her life."

Alex tightened his jaw. She was right. She was almost always right, and it drove him crazy. "You're out of line."

Maggie's cheeks turned pink. "I have to speak honestly. If I can't stay on to take care of her, at least I can try to help you see she has needs which you *cannot* ignore. She needs *you*. And maybe you need her."

Alex tapped his fingers on the desktop and looked out the window. "Thank you for your input," he said shortly, then looked down at his papers. Parenting was the most awesome responsibility in his life and he'd had more than enough criticism about his handling of it. "Please send my secretary in on your way out."

"I'm not going."

He looked up at her, surprised. "What?" The corner of his mouth ticked. This woman was amazing. He'd never seen someone with so much gall. He really admired it.

"I'm *sure* you have connections somewhere in Washington," Maggie said. "I'm not leaving this room until you agree to help me stay at least three more months. Kate needs more time. *I* need more time."

"I wish I could help you, I really do," he said, and meant it. The house was going to be awfully quiet after Maggie packed her opinions and left. It was regrettable. "There's nothing more I can do."

Before Maggie could respond, the door creaked open behind her and Kate walked in. Her dark, moss green eyes were wide but unafraid. Not for the first time, Alex wondered at how much Maggie and Kate looked like mother and daughter. It had to be the light hair, he decided, or the eyes. Strange, since neither he nor his ex-wife had those particular characteristics.

"Sorry to innerupt," Kate said, her sweet voice clear.

"What do you need?" Alex asked, feeling suddenly self-conscious. A boardroom full of high-powered executives was nothing compared to the intimidation from this one big-eyed five-year-old.

The tense moment of silence that followed was punctuated by a phone ringing in another room.

Kate looked at her father briefly then rushed to Maggie. "Maggie?" she asked in a hushed voice.

"Yes, darling?" Maggie answered, with a glance toward Alex.

"Can you put Ariel's head back on?" Kate held a decapitated doll head in her small hand. "It came off again."

Maggie laughed and knelt in front of Kate. "Of course, sweetheart. Did she fall off the horse again?"

Kate nodded enthusiastically. "They were racing. Ariel won."

"Good for her." Maggie took the doll head. "Remember, because we've put it back on so many times, it's going to be loose."

Alex could have sworn he heard her add, "I'm feeling that way myself."

She pressed the head onto the body Kate pulled from her jumper pocket and heard it snap in place. "There you are. Good as new." She held out the doll, whose head tilted slightly to the right. "I feel like Dr. Frankenstein."

Kate's smile was as bright as morning, something *he* rarely saw. Maggie's effect on her was truly astonishing. Where once his daughter had been sullen and constantly miserable, now she was open and relaxed.

Maggie was right—he couldn't let her go. For *Kate's* sake he couldn't let her go.

But the only possible solution was so…radical.

"Thanks." Kate beamed. "I *knew* you could fix it. You're the best!"

Maggie wrapped her arms around the small form and Alex noticed she blinked back tears. "*You're* the best."

"No, *you're* the best." Kate giggled at their familiar game.

Maggie pulled back and straightened to her full five feet eight inches. She ran her hands across her slender hips to straighten her skirt, and Alex felt a tightening in his chest. "Daddy and I are talking right now. Go on up to your playroom and I'll be along in a few minutes. Why don't you dress Betsy in the blue ball gown? Ariel can wear the pink. They'll have a party this afternoon, how's that?"

"Great!" Kate turned to dash from the room then stopped and turned back. "Bye, Father."

He was startled by her attention to him. "Bye…Kate. I'll see you later."

Maggie closed the door behind her. "I can't stand to leave her like this." She placed her hands on her hips and shifted.

Alex shifted, too, then took a long breath. Her short denim skirt had folded up at the thigh when she bent down to Kate but when she stood it didn't go all the way back down despite her efforts. Only about four inches of material were between his gaze and her— He couldn't think about it. "I agree it would be best for you to stay with Kate." He cleared his throat. "But the only—"

"I know, I know, you have no choice." She threw her hands up and took a step to the side. The lean muscles in her legs flexed. "You're going to hire another nanny, and another one after that, and another—"

"Stop. Please. Let me think." He pressed his hands down on the desk, pushed his chair back and leaned back in it. He gazed at Maggie in front of him. There was a spirit in her eyes that had never been in Sandra's.

His jaw tightened at the thought of his deceased ex-wife. How many nannies had *she* gone through before Kate had come to live with him? Sandra hadn't worked—she'd lived off his substantial alimony payments—yet she had somehow found it necessary to employ a complete staff, including full-time care for Kate.

Kate needed consistency, Maggie was right about that. In fact, it was long overdue. *But what should I do?* he asked himself. *How far can I go to provide it?*

He closed his eyes hard and opened them to find Maggie, standing before him, like the answer to his question.

The intercom on his desk buzzed. "Alex, Anna Christianson is on the phone again," his secretary's voice informed him.

"Take a message," he growled, trying to ignore Maggie's eyes on him. Wannabe socialite, Anna Christianson was relentless in her pursuit of him—or, more specifically, his money—and everyone knew it. It was a fact he found very embarrassing. "Get rid of her."

"Okay, Alex, but this *is* the third call today, you know. Is there something specific I can tell her?"

"Tell her anything. Tell her I've...gotten married." He heaved a breath and met Maggie's eyes, then looked away quickly. "Tell her I'm on an extended vacation. Tell her anything." He released his hand from the intercom. "Please don't lecture me on honesty now," he said to Maggie.

"I wasn't going to."

He ran a hand through his hair. "Oh, it's in there somewhere."

"What is?"

"A recrimination."

She lowered her chin. "Is this your guilty conscience speaking?" Her eyes looked truly luminous.

Interesting trick of the light, Alex forced himself to conclude. "Guilty? What do I have to feel guilty about?" The minute the words were out he knew he was going to regret asking.

She turned the corners of her mouth down and shrugged. "Maybe you're feeling guilty because you're not willing to take proper care of your child."

He stood abruptly and the chair trembled behind him. "Maggie, the fact is I'm busy, now and always. There are too many distractions as it is." He glanced disgustedly at the intercom. "I have to work in order to keep Kate well fed and clothed. I wouldn't be doing her any favors if I gave up my job."

"You don't have to work twenty-four hours a day."

He hesitated. "The single most important thing I can do is *provide* for my child." He spoke low and slowly. Every word held equal weight. "Not every parent has that priority and, *believe me,* their children suffer for it."

"I agree that basic financial security is important, but believe *me* it's easy to err in the opposite direction. All I'm suggesting is a little moderation."

"I have no time for moderation. Or for anything much but work. That's why I hired you."

"Are you trying to tell me that you can't *afford* to take a little time off?" Maggie looked around her at the opulent office; the leather chairs, stone fireplace, Oriental carpets. "This is one room in a mansion of at least forty. The property alone is worth enough to support several ordinary people for life. You have done quite well for yourself and for Harrison Satellite Networks. I won't believe for a moment that you *need* to spend every single day of your life at work."

He followed her gaze around the room then held it with his own. "I don't need to justify any of this to you. If you'll excuse me now, I have something else to do."

"That's typical, I guess," she said, almost under her breath. She didn't move, though inside she trembled.

"What's typical?" he asked, turning back to face her.

Maggie shrugged. "You. Men like you. If there's a problem that can't be solved with money you turn away from it and pretend it doesn't exist at all."

He shook his head as he went through the door. "That's your assessment of me?" he said over his shoulder as he started down the stairs, with Maggie close behind.

"Part of it."

"I'm flattered." He opened the door to his home gym and went in.

She slipped in as the door was closing. "You also have a dreadful tendency toward sarcasm," she said pointedly.

He stopped and faced her. "Tell me, Miss Weller, have you *ever* had an unexpressed opinion?"

She looked at him steadily. "I'm having one right now."

There was a moment of shivering silence. Then, to her utter surprise he laughed. The creases framing his smile gave him a boyish look that Maggie tried to ignore. The laugh changed his whole face, if only for a moment. It threw her off more than anything he could have said.

"Okay." He turned, then paused at the door and looked at her for a moment before turning. "Let's talk about you staying. For Kate's sake and for your sake and, God help me, for my sake." Not that he had any personal reason to want her to stay. It was all about Kate.

Walking past her, he slipped his jacket off, then draped it over a wooden valet in the changing room. The crisp white fabric of his button-down shirt formed against his powerful back. He opened a drawer and took out sweatpants and a T-shirt. "You'll excuse me a minute?"

Noticing where she stood, Maggie backed up a step and closed the door. "Did you say for *your* sake?" she asked.

There was a pause of several seconds before he replied, "What's good for Kate is good for me, isn't it?"

"It could make things *easier* for you."

"Easier? I don't think anything good comes easy." He stepped out of the changing room, wearing worn-out sweatpants and a T-shirt.

Maggie swallowed as her eyes roamed over Alex Harrison's body. She'd never seem him so bare. For the first time she saw a pale jagged scar that cut across his muscular shoulder. It gave him a ruggedness that she didn't generally attribute to him. She touched her cheek. It felt warm. "Life isn't only hard work, Alex." Her voice quivered.

He seemed unaware of her perusal. "So you say," he replied, lying down under the bench press. He released the bar and began repetitions, well-defined muscles flexing under smooth skin, up and down, making her think of the power in those arms, the strength his embrace might have. "Maggie, there is only one way I can think of for you to stay in this country," he continued as he rested the bar on its stand and shook his hands.

"You've thought of something?" She forced her gaze to his face and tried to stare impassively down at him. "What?"

He turned his head toward her. "It's pretty extreme. In fact, it may be too extreme."

"You're not proposing that I should stay in this country illegally?"

He met her eyes, then lifted the bar again. "No, of course not." He lowered it to his chest. His biceps bulged again as his skin began to sheen with a light sweat. "I'm proposing something entirely different."

She swallowed and kept her eyes on his face. "What is it?"

He finished a count of twelve and set the bar down again, an unreadable expression on his face. "If you married an American you could stay in the country with a green card. When enough time passed, you could apply for citizenship."

"Who on earth am I going to—"

"Me." He sat up and rubbed his palms on his sweat-pants, then met her stunned gaze.

She couldn't have heard him correctly. "That's impossible."

He looked back at her, the full force of his concentration powerful and compelling. "No, it's not."

"Are you serious?"

"Yes. Then you could stay on full-time through the summer, then move out when Kate starts first grade in the fall. Get a place of your own nearby so you can stay involved with Kate. She won't need full-time care then anyway. You get your green card and Kate doesn't have the shock of breaking in another nanny. Seems to me this arrangement would be mutually beneficial.''

Mutually beneficial. Alex Harrison was offering her marriage as a cold-as-marble business proposition, nothing more. But what in the world could she expect? ''I can't do that.''

He crossed his arms in front of him. The muscles beneath his gleaming skin rippled with the movement. ''Why not?''

''I can't imagine being in a marriage that wasn't real.''

He shook his head. ''*Real* marriages don't work. That's been proven over and over again by countless unhappy people. Business arrangements, on the other hand, generally do because both parties go into it with an understanding about the outcome.''

''Meaning…?''

''Everyone wins. Kate would have consistency, she'd have the very best care, she'd have *you*, which is what she clearly wants. You, on the other hand, would have an opportunity to gain financial security before returning to your country, if you decide to go back.''

''I'd rather forge my opportunities for myself,'' Maggie countered hotly, his detachment suddenly irritating.

A new look came into his eyes. ''You're not very practical.''

''That may be true. But if I agree to some plan so I can stay, for Kate's sake as well as my own, I don't want you thinking I was doing it for financial gain.''

''Why would you care what I think? I'm proposing the plan.''

She stiffened. ''I care about Kate.''

''So do I. So stay. For a while.''

She sighed, looking into those cryptic blue eyes. "As your wife?"

He held up a hand. "My wife in name. Kate's nanny in fact. A simple business arrangement that solves all short-term problems." Alex reached out and touched Maggie's arm. "Is it so horrifying?" he asked. "Am I?"

An electric current passed between them at the unexpected words and touch. Maggie was aware of a quickening of her pulse.

"And how do you benefit from it?" she asked.

He looked into Maggie's eyes. "I want Kate to be happy. I think this would make her happy."

Maggie narrowed her eyes. "Is that all?"

He let out a breath. "Okay, to be totally frank, being a married man might make my life a little easier in other ways. Success tends to attract a certain type of woman—"

"Gold diggers?" Maggie supplied.

"That's one term for them. Anyway, I could do without the aggravation of three calls a day from the Anna Christiansons out there."

Maggie thought for a moment, then nodded. "If I move out at the end of the summer—"

"Marital discord," Alex said. "We'll say we're trying to work it out."

"Even if that would work, I'm not sure it justifies a marriage."

"Think about it." He gave a brief smile that warmed his face. "Please think it over. I believe it's the only way."

Holding his gaze, she reached for the chair behind her, found it, pulled it toward her and sat down. "I can't believe I'm considering this."

"It's a very sensible offer." He gave a half shrug and his voice softened. "And as you so persuasively pointed out, it's vitally important for Kate."

For several long seconds they sat in silence. There was a lot of merit in what he said. After all, this was not meant to be a romantic proposal. Could she separate her feelings? Could she, even for a short time, lock herself in marriage with this man and accept that it wasn't real?

Finally she said, "If it weren't for Kate I'd walk away from this ridiculous conversation." *And if it weren't for the fact that I need to stay in this country so I can earn the money to send home where there is almost no employment.* She didn't want to admit it, but she was very tempted to take him up on his offer for her own selfish reasons.

"If it weren't for Kate we wouldn't be having this conversation at all." Alex stood. "I'll need an answer today and I've got a meeting downtown in two hours. Let me know, Maggie."

An hour later Maggie and Alex were back in the office where the whole conversation began, he in his chair behind the desk, she in the one opposite. Alex had his closing argument perfectly prepared.

"...so by marrying me, I'll offer you the chance to complete your Montessori certification. Also, you'll be able to apply for citizenship so that after we separate you can remain in this country as a legal citizen. You can vote, collect benefits and take a teaching job anywhere you want freely, without restrictions."

"I don't even know how long one has to be a resident before being eligible for citizenship," Maggie said.

"Three years. I'd expect you to live in the area during that time so you could be available to Kate when she's not in school. Naturally I will compensate you for your time.''

Three years. This was no small commitment. Maggie raised a skeptical eyebrow. ''And what happens to Kate after the three years?'' *And what happens to us in the meantime?*

''We'll have to agree now that you'll continue to be part of her life, at least to some degree. I'll make it financially possible for you to visit with her whenever the two of you would like.''

''But what about between visits?''

''I'll be here much of the time, but I'll make sure there's a housekeeper here at all times as well.''

Maggie struggled not to roll her eyes. ''Oh, well, as long as you have an hour or so a week—''

The look he gave her stopped her cold. ''If we're going to keep arguing like this, maybe we should forget the whole thing.''

Maggie saw he meant it. Suddenly the answer was clear. She realized with vague irony that she had shoved her attraction to him aside. At that moment, the man's very coldness made her feel that it would be possible to marry him in the legal sense only. The glimpses of sensitivity she'd seen were enough to make her believe that, with a little bit of time and understanding, perhaps he would see the close relationship he could have with Kate. Without vanity, Maggie believed that she was the one person who could help this come to fruition.

And that was as noble and worthy a cause as she'd ever had. Whether Alex Harrison realized it or not, he had given her much more than an opportunity to finish school or get a good job. He'd given her a challenge that, if she succeeded, could change all their lives. But for the better? Maggie didn't know the answer to that.

"Let's not forget about it, Alex," she said aloud. "I accept the challenge." She took a deep breath, met his eyes and held out a hand to seal the deal. "You've just bought yourself a wife. When's our wedding?"

Chapter Two

"I beg your pardon?"

"I'll do it," Maggie said. "It seems best for everyone involved, as you said." Her eyes were brighter than usual and her face had grown paler. She looked like a porcelain doll, except that there was nothing fragile about her. She was willowy but solidly built. She was beautifully built, as a matter of fact. "But I think we have to have an understanding about this."

"We'll have a formal agreement, of course." It was a lesson he'd learned from bitter experience. "A prenuptial agreement that addresses both of our concerns. What are your yours?"

"Several things." She drew a breath. "As you know I had an entire hour to think about this. I made some notes." She took a folded piece of paper out of her pocket. "First, finances. Will I continue to get a weekly check or did you have something else in mind?"

"I could establish an account in your name and arrange for automatic deposits according to your spending.''

She sucked air in through her teeth. ''I'd rather take care of my own economics.''

''Fine.'' He hesitated, then wrote something down on a piece of paper. ''I can't very well keep my wife on salary but I can call it a monthly stipend for your personal use. Direct deposit would be more subtle.'' He slid the paper to her.

Maggie looked at the paper. ''But that's considerably more than I'm earning now,'' she said. ''If my duties aren't going to change, I don't think it's appropriate for my salary to change.''

He raised an eyebrow. ''Are you arguing against a *raise?*''

Her look hardened slightly. ''I have no intention of taking advantage of you. All I want is what's fair.''

He tapped his pen against the pad. ''This is a somewhat more constant occupation. Don't forget you'll be my wife as well as Kate's supervisor.''

She lowered her chin. ''That sounds ominous. What does being your wife entail that warrants so much more money? Besides scaring off gold diggers?''

He shrugged. ''Regular wifely duty type things. Nothing much.''

She frowned for a moment, then her eyes widened. ''Oh, no.'' She stood up and shook her head. ''No, no.''

''What?''

''Is this about *sex?*''

He lowered his brows and tried to keep from laughing. ''Who mentioned sex?''

She put her hands on her hips. ''You increased my salary because I will also have to perform wifely duties. Do you mean you expect me to sleep with you?''

"Did I say 'perform'?" He pushed away the thought of her shapely legs wrapped around him. "I don't think I said 'perform.'"

She threw her hands up. "I don't know what you said, but it certainly sounded like an improper proposition to me."

He looked at her calmly. "Maggie, are you prepared to take money for such...services?"

Her face flushed red. "Certainly not!"

"Then why do you assume I'm prepared to pay for them?"

She eyed him for a moment, then her mouth quirked into a smile. "Okay, you have a good point. I leapt to a conclusion. How about if you tell me what you meant by 'wifely duty' and I'll reserve judgment. For a moment."

He studied his Mont Blanc fountain pen. "When news gets out that I'm married there will be business functions now and then that you'll be invited to attend with me. Now, I can probably get you out of most of them, but I can't guarantee you'll never have to come along."

"Business functions?"

He nodded and put the pen down.

"Of course." She met his eyes. "I don't have any problem with that."

"Good." He tapped his fingers on the armrests of his chair, amazed that the conversation was really happening. It wasn't difficult for him to consider marriage as a business proposition—after all, there were a million legal ways to protect himself. But it was another thing to think of Maggie as his wife and remember that it was *strictly* business...with only a fraction of the usual marital benefits.

She sat down again and crossed her long legs. Inside, Alex groaned. "So when you talked about my role as your wife and said this was a legal marriage, you meant...?"

"Legal means legal...in the eyes of the state," Alex said, glancing at her long slender legs. He returned his gaze to her eyes, but not without a momentary pause at her exquisite lips. "You will keep your own room."

She raised her chin and looked at him for a moment before nodding. "Okay. So we're agreed. No...marital interaction."

He didn't mean to hesitate but suddenly he had to swallow. "Of course not. No sex. Not with one another at any rate."

She looked up sharply. "Do you have someone in mind?" Her words were unexpectedly crisp.

"Do you?" he countered.

"I'm not sure that's a question you should be asking me."

"Why not?"

She shifted in her chair. "Because I'm not sure it's any of your business."

"You asked me."

"Well, yes, but...but I'm not the one who brought it up in the first place."

There was no one else in her life. That was a relief. If Maggie had been interested in someone, it would really have muddied things up. Where Kate was concerned, that was. "Okay, we'll make a deal. We'll have a no-questions-asked policy." Now he felt safe proposing this. "Discretion is the only requirement."

"Another deal," Maggie mused. She reached up and pulled her long golden hair back from her face.

Alex watched and swallowed hard. Every once in

awhile he'd seen her do that and each time it struck him how much she looked like Grace Kelly. Funny, when he was young, he'd seen *Rear Window* and developed a tremendous crush on Grace Kelly. He'd forgotten that until just now.

"Do you agree?" he asked, after a silence that he knew had gone on too long.

"Yes." Her chest rose with a deep breath and the buttons of her blouse strained slightly. "So how do you want to do it?"

His heart skipped a beat. "Do...?"

"The marriage," she answered quickly. "The actual ceremony or what have you."

"Ah, well." He straightened in his chair and shuffled some papers on his desk. "I suppose we'll go to the courthouse."

"The courthouse. Fine." Maggie swallowed. "When?"

He tapped his fingertips on the desk, then steepled his fingers in front of his face. For some reason he didn't want to appear too anxious. "I'll have to check my schedule and get back to you on that."

Some expression flitted across her features, but too quickly for Alex to identify it. She heaved a sigh and regarded him for a moment. There was such a look of intelligence in her eyes. Alex found it disconcerting. As if she could see right through him.

"Fine," she said, breaking his thoughts. "But I don't suppose we should wait too long." She nodded toward the paper listing her visa expiration.

"No," he agreed. "I just have to make a few calls and then I'll have my secretary make the arrangements." He added, "You do realize that an immigration review board will want to set up a time to interview us.''

She blinked. ''Why?''

''To make sure our marriage is real. This *is* an eleventh hour move, after all.''

''How are they going to confirm that?''

''It's my understanding that they'll ask us a series of questions about each other and our life together. We'll have to spend some time together preparing.''

''Should I be worried?''

''I don't think so. It's like any other test. We'll just make sure we're prepared.'' He hesitated. ''Do you have any other points to clear up?'' He nodded toward the paper she'd brought along.

She glanced at it. ''How do we handle...the end? In three years.''

''At the end of three years, I propose to give you a lump sum, again for your personal use. I imagine that you'll use it to establish yourself as single again.'' He pulled the pad over, wrote, then passed the paper to her.

She took it and gasped. ''Are you sure you wrote this correctly?'' She held it up for him to see.

He didn't bother to look. ''It's not enough?'' He poised his pen. ''I'll only go up another ten thousand.''

''*Another* ten thousand?'' She shook her head. ''It looks like you'll be eager to be rid of me.''

He couldn't imagine it. ''I only want to be fair. That's the way I do all my business.''

''Then it's no wonder you're so successful.'' There was a hard edge to her voice. ''But *this*—'' she looked at the paper ''—isn't necessary. Not for me.''

Alex looked at her sharply, hating the clutch in his gut. ''You don't like me, do you?''

''Do you care whether I do or not?''

He *couldn't* care. But how could he explain that to her? "It's not imperative."

She eyed him in silence, then asked, "What if one of us wants to get out of the marriage early?"

He went cold. "Is that a possibility?" he asked in a tone more sharp than he'd intended.

She met his eyes. "I don't know, is it? What if you fall in love and want to marry someone else?"

He grimaced. "That's not going to happen. For me. And if we make this deal and *you* want to marry someone else, you're going to have to wait until the end of this term. Kate *must* be settled in a new situation before you leave."

"Naturally."

"Furthermore, you *must* agree to stay in touch with her afterward. I know it's a big commitment, but otherwise, there's no deal." He watched Maggie's eyes. "Can you agree to that?"

"Of course." She straightened her shoulders. "I wouldn't have it any other way. It's even on my list." She held it out halfheartedly.

"Good. Then I'll have my lawyer draw up a contract and bring it to you for a signature."

"A *contract?*" She looked astonished. "Don't you trust me?"

Trust. That wasn't a word he wanted to discuss with a woman. "It's just good business," he hedged. "It helps everyone remember their objectives."

She nodded stiffly. "Very well. Now if you'll excuse me, I have to see to Kate."

"Right." He watched her turn to go, then had another thought. "Maggie?"

She turned around. "Yes?"

Their eyes locked for just a moment. "Since you're

going up to Kate," Alex said slowly, "maybe you ought to tell her about our plans now."

A moment passed. "You want *me* to tell her?"

Alex raised an eyebrow. "Is that a problem?"

"You want me to tell her *alone?*"

He shrugged. "That's what I hired you for."

"You can't mean that."

Lord, he'd set her off again. He didn't have time to wade through her inventory of synonyms for *I-don't-approve-of-what-you're-doing*. "Let's cut to the chase, here. Do you have a problem with telling her?"

Maggie crossed her arms in front of her and regarded him with a look of incredulity that made him extremely uncomfortable. "Surely *you* intend to tell her this news."

So that was it. "You're the one who is with her all the time."

"You're her father!" Maggie returned, seeming exasperated for having to point out something so obvious.

"I know that," he answered, impatient over having to acknowledge something so obvious. He picked up a pen and tipped it back and forth between his fingers. "Am I to gather that you think I should speak with Kate myself?"

She bit down on her lower lip and nodded, with exaggerated patience.

"Okay, I'll do it later."

She opened her mouth to speak, then closed it again.

"You had something else to say?" Alex asked.

"On second thought, maybe we should do it together."

He dropped the pen on the desk and it clattered onto the floor. The woman was amazing. "Maggie, have you always been this impossible or do I bring it out in you?''

She looked at him steadily, her green eyes dark and sharp. "Oh, I've always been this way," she said, completely earnest. "It's just me."

"I'll keep that in mind."

"See you upstairs," she said with a smile. She'd caught him, gained the upper hand, if only for a moment. What was worse, she knew it. He could tell.

"Wait." He had to say something, anything, to regain control of this relationship.

Maggie looked at him expectantly.

"Please tell Kate I'd like to speak to her at—" he glanced at his watch "—three o'clock." He eyed Maggie coolly. "I'll expect you to be there as well."

She nodded then turned and left, closing the heavy oak door behind her with a solid thud.

A tremor ran through his chest and he took a deep breath. He stared after her for a long time. Damn her attractiveness, he thought. She was integral to the next few years running smoothly. Yet attraction to her would cause too many problems.

He picked up a pencil and drew circles on the pad in front of him.

Physical attraction was one complication he was going to have to ignore. There were far more pressing complications that took precedence. Marlene Shaw, for example. His former mother-in-law was trying to take custody of Kate away from him. Knowing what he did of his ex-wife, Sandra's, upbringing, and how she had turned out to be of less-than-sterling character, Alex was willing to protect Kate from that fate with whatever it took. Marlene was an ambitious, demanding woman who, like her daughter, wanted what she wanted at all costs. Unfortunately she had lived with Kate during the two years after the divorce. Now with Alex as a hard-working bachelor she had some leverage in the court's eye.

Maggie could change all of that. With a wife at his side, a wife who was devoted to Kate, he would no longer have to worry about Marlene Shaw. She would have no more ammunition. And Kate would have the best of care.

Meanwhile, he also wouldn't have to worry about other women pursuing him anymore, he thought without conceit. The undesirables would leave him alone if he was married. The others…well, there weren't any others, so he didn't have to worry about that, either.

There were a lot of practical advantages to his being married.

That was what he had to focus on, not his body's attraction to Maggie.

The circles he drew became tighter and darker.

Maggie Weller—soon to be Harrison—was, as Alex's late mother would have termed her, "a pistol." She certainly outspunked any woman Alex had ever known. But the funny thing was, he liked that. He admired her for it.

And she was so highly principled. If Sandra had been half as principled as Maggie, half as honest, then maybe their marriage wouldn't have been such a disaster.

Thank God Maggie wasn't like Sandra.

Now if she could pass on any of that confidence, integrity, even self-righteousness, to Kate he would be grateful. He didn't want Kate to suffer because of insecurities and he never wanted her to fear her father's temper, the way he had. After all, Kate had to live with Alex, and Alex was his father's son. If it was true that the apple didn't fall too far from the tree, she might as well learn early not to need him, lest he should let her down.

He stopped scribbling on the paper.

And so he would have to remember not to need her, too, not to get too attached. For her sake.

The pencil snapped in his hand.

Half an hour later, Alex decided to phone his former mother-in-law and get it over with. He flipped through the Rolodex file on his desk until he came to the name he sought: Marlene Shaw. With one final deep breath for strength, he picked up the phone and dialed.

They made it through the pleasantries quickly, then Alex got directly to the point. "I'm getting married in a couple of weeks."

There was a thick pause. "Is that right?" Marlene asked icily. "To whom?"

Alex could tell from the stiffness of her voice that she was already trying to determine whether this was going to help or hinder her custody case. "To Margaret Weller."

"Margaret Weller," the older woman repeated, "Margaret We—" There was an audible gasp. "Surely you're not talking about the nanny!"

"The same."

"That's impossible."

"I don't think so."

"She's a servant!"

"That's not exactly the way I think of things, Marlene. Kate couldn't ask for a better stepmother."

"But Kate...why, she needs family. There's no substitute for blood, Alex. No one could be better for her than her own flesh and blood. Some outsider can't give her that.''

He let a moment of silence linger after her outburst, then said mildly, ''She has that. I'm her father, you remember.''

The derisive snort on the line was answer enough.

''And now she's going to have a stepmother who loves her, too.'' He waited a beat. ''So I trust I won't be hearing from you again about custody.''

''You do, do you? Well, think again. We don't even know where that woman's from, what her background is. She could be a criminal for all we know about her—''

Alex shifted his grip on the receiver. ''My people screened her before I hired her. So drop it, Marlene. You know you don't have a case, and I'd really rather not have to describe your schemes to my fiancée.''

''Isn't that why you're marrying her?'' Marlene shot back. ''To keep me from my grandchild?''

''Of course not,'' he snapped, unable to quell a small tremor of guilt. ''I'm marrying her because I want Kate to have a good family, a *rational* environment.''

''I see.'' Marlene drew out the last word. ''But you're mistaken if you think this will help your case.''

''Your attempts to get custody don't hold water,'' he lied. ''They never have. You have no grounds.''

''Have you forgotten that I lived with Sandra and Kate? I practically raised that child!''

Cold washed over Alex. ''We both know that's not true.''

''Oh, but it is.'' Her voice echoed her daughter's cruel sarcasm.

Alex swallowed. His lawyer had told him it was extremely unlikely she could win a custody battle, but recent headlines and news stories about custody hearings had made Alex nervous. Stranger things than a grandmother winning guardianship had happened. Besides, even his lawyer had acknowledged that Marlene's having lived with Kate and Sandra had given her a tiny bit of leverage.

"I've got a call holding." Alex's mouth was dry. "I just wanted to let you know that I would be marrying again and that Kate will have a stepmother. One who will love her and take excellent care of her. I thought that would be important to you."

"That girl is a foreigner, isn't she?" Marlene snapped, as though Alex hadn't spoken at all.

He let out a weary sigh. "She's British."

"How very convenient for her. Of course you know all *she* wants is to become an American. They *all* want to become Americans."

He increased his grip on the phone. "I'm hanging up now. It was a pleasure talking with you, as always."

His tone was unmistakably dismissive, but she still managed to add, "This isn't over, Alex. Margaret Weller has got a few things to prove to me, I can tell you. I shall be calling the British Embassy and U.S. immigration authorities right away to have them look into the matter."

He knew he shouldn't ask but he couldn't help it. "Matter?"

"The matter of this hasty wedding, of course." Her voice was syrupy with malice. "I'd hate for *Kate* to be caught in the middle of an immigration scandal."

Chapter Three

Maggie and Kate sat on Kate's bed, playing with dolls when Alex came looking for them.

"You can't keep me from going to that ball," Kate squeaked in a high, false voice. She waved her doll in another doll's face. "The prince wants *me* to go!"

Alex smiled at the already-small voice raised further in imitation of another, and leaned against the door frame to watch.

"I'll lock you in the attic," Maggie returned, in a cartoon-bad-guy voice that made Alex chuckle to himself. "And your little mouse friends, too."

"No! No!" Kate bounced the doll away, pogo-stick fashion. "I won't stay!"

"Aaargh!" Maggie's doll fell on its face in the covers. "I can't move! *Helllp!*" She dropped the doll down, then looked up, smiling, and took another doll. "I'm here now," the doll said with Maggie's help. "Your fairy godmother will save you."

"No, go away!"

Maggie looked surprised. "But I'm your fairy godmother. I'm good."

Still talking in the doll's voice, Kate said, "Good mothers aren't any better than bad ones. They leave you. Go away!"

The doll in Maggie's hand trembled ever so slightly. "But I won't leave you."

"Yes, you will! Mommies leave." Kate hurled her doll against the one in Maggie's hand and fell silent.

Maggie put the dolls aside gently and moved a bit closer to Kate. "You don't really believe that, do you?"

Kate didn't meet her eyes. "It's true. My mommy left. Now I don't have a mother at all."

Maggie looked choked up. With absolutely no idea how to help the situation, Alex cleared his throat and walked in. "What are you two doing?" he asked, as casually as he could.

Maggie looked at him, composure sweeping her features. "Well, I'm glad you're here. Kate just asked me an important question. She wanted to know why her mommy had to leave her." She focused her attention on Kate. "Your mommy didn't want to leave you, darling, but she had to."

"Because she died?" Kate asked.

Alex winced at her bluntness.

"Yes," Maggie said, with what sounded like an effort. "The truth is that sometimes things happen that we don't understand right away."

Kate looked down and said in a horribly quiet voice. "I understand. She died because I was naughty."

Maggie's sharp intake of breath echoed Alex's own feelings. "Why do you say that, Kate?" he asked her gently.

Kate looked up with tear-filled eyes. "I was too

noisy. I played too loud. Grandma told me if I didn't be quiet then Mommy was going to get sicker, and I *tried* to be as quiet as a mouse..."

Alex couldn't let her go on. "It wasn't your fault," he said, a little too gruffly.

She started at the tone of his voice and something in him stung.

"No," Maggie soothed in a voice that belied the shock on her face, "it wasn't your fault."

"But grandma said—"

"Grandma was wrong," Alex growled. And the witch wanted custody of Kate! Anger seared him and he looked to Maggie for tempering.

Maggie met his eyes and nodded, rubbing her hand across Kate's back. "You did nothing wrong, darling, nothing at all. Mummy died because she was sick, and that was terribly sad for you. But I don't believe for a moment that your Mummy left you entirely. I think her love is with you all the time. You'll have that forever." She laid a hand across Kate's heart. "Right here."

"Do you really think so?"

"I know it."

Kate smiled, despite the tears still wet on her cheeks. "You're very smart, Maggie."

Maggie lifted her hand and ruffled Kate's hair. "No, darling, I'm just old." She laughed.

"And as for noise," Alex said, "we won't have any quiet children in this house."

Kate looked stricken. "You won't?"

What had he said? The child looked terrified. "You can make tons of noise." He gave an uneasy smile, trying to wipe the fear from his daughter's face.

The tears started anew. "Or else what? Are you going to send me away? Where would I go?"

Alex's eyes widened and he looked desperately to
Maggie, who was watching him in silence. She wasn't
going to help this time. "Never," he said. "I'll never
send you away." He moved toward Kate and reached
for her, pulling her into an awkward embrace. "I promise. You're going no further than our own backyard."

Small hands clutched at his back. "Even if I don't
make a lot of noise?"

"I'll never send you away," he repeated, embar-
rassed at the choked sound of his own voice. "No matter what. And that's why Maggie's here. She's going to
stay."

Kate pulled back and looked at Maggie. "Will you
stay *forever*?"

"I'll stay as long as you need me to." Maggie gave
her a warm smile. "But remember you can always
count on your daddy, too. Always."

"Okay." Kate sniffed. She turned her liquid eyes to
Alex and smiled, sending his heart tumbling. The responsibility for this child, this little heart, was an awesome one. He'd denied the pull of it for months now,
but he couldn't do it any longer.

Alex realized the conversation was over. Maggie had
handled it perfectly, with just the right lightness of
touch. The woman was a godsend, there was no doubt
about it. He watched her hand stroking Kate's hair and
felt his chest tighten with relief. Relief that Kate was in
such loving and capable hands.

Maggie had proven once again how much more adept
she was at handling his child than he was. He hoped to
God she would still go through with the marriage once
she found out about Marlene's threats.

She caught his eye and mouthed the word *now?* and
gestured toward her left ring finger.

He gave a small shake of his head, then turned to his daughter. "Kate, could you excuse us for a minute?"

"Okay…" Kate looked to Maggie, seeming a bit puzzled.

"I have to talk to Daddy for a moment," Maggie said. "I'll be right back."

Outside in the hall, she turned to Alex.

He took a step toward her, closing the bedroom door behind him.

Even though there was room, neither one of them stepped away to widen the space between them.

"Have you changed your mind already?" she asked him lightly.

"Yes."

She took a breath and her gaze flitted from his chest to his eyes. "Oh?"

"About the ceremony." His voice was a hoarse whisper in the dimly lit hall. "We need to have something more than just the courthouse."

"Why?"

He hesitated. "Don't you have family you want to invite?"

"My mother…isn't much of a traveler. Though she sends her best wishes." She leaned against the wall, but it added only an inch or two between them. "I called her before our contract discussion. She thinks you're a very lucky man, actually." She smiled.

"I am," he said, and at that moment meant it. Even though he knew this relationship—this *marriage*—was to be different, for just a moment he felt like the luckiest man on earth. It was crazy.

Maggie looked at him. Her green eyes were wide and tentative. "I didn't mean…I wasn't soliciting compliments." She dampened her parted lips.

"I know you weren't." He tried to stop the rush of desire that came over him, but couldn't.

"But that was nice, thank you."

He paused, then decided to say what he felt. "I meant it. The way you handle things." He looked at Kate's closed door, then back at Maggie. "I don't see how I could do this without you." He hesitated again, wondering at the depth of his meaning or if he was a fool to admit it to her. "I'm just glad I don't have to try."

"But you were ready to just find another nanny," Maggie said softly, still holding his gaze.

Maybe he could find another nanny, but he couldn't find another Maggie—another woman who would give him such a hard time or who could make that hard time so damned enjoyable—so easily. Funny, he'd never quite been able to admit that before. Maybe it was because he always knew she would be leaving.

And now he knew she was staying.

As she stood before him he realized with an awkward awareness that she was quite beautiful. Beautiful enough to make him stumble over his words like a schoolboy. "You couldn't be easily replaced," he said.

"Yesterday you were ready to do just that." She challenged him with her eyes.

"Yesterday I thought I had to. Besides, you know you're more than just a nanny."

A slight flush darkened her cheeks. "Oh?"

"Kate really loves you."

Soot-dark lashes lowered like a curtain.

"Maggie."

She met his eyes. Before he realized what he was doing, Alex reached his hand to her cheek, and slowly rubbed his thumb across the smooth blushing skin.

She didn't move, and her gaze remained fixed on his.

She wasn't going to leave. She was staying.

Alex slid his hand behind her head and gently pulled her toward him. Their lips met and fire shot to his extremities. For a long moment they didn't move, then Maggie's lips parted under his and he nudged his tongue into her mouth.

Her hands rose tentatively to his chest and he moved his other hand to the small of her back. Hunger for her burned quick and bright inside of Alex, despite the fact that he knew—he *knew*—he shouldn't be doing this. Only half an hour before, they had agreed *not* to do this. He ran his tongue along her upper lip marveling at the blaze of sensation within him.

Suddenly Maggie stopped. She drew back, flushed and a little out of breath. "What was that?" she said, perhaps to him, perhaps to herself.

"A kiss."

"I know that. But…us?" She took a step away from him, looking everywhere but at him. "That's not appropriate for us. It can't happen again."

He stared at her for a moment in silence, taking in the fiery eyes, the cheeks still flushed with passion, the full lips swollen from their kiss. There was nothing he could say, he knew she was right but he couldn't voice his agreement.

So he gave a slight incline of the head. "I apologize," he said, without an ounce of sincerity.

She obviously knew it because it was a long, narrow look she gave him before saying, "You were about to say something about the wedding." She drew herself up and met his eyes boldly. "Why do you want to have a bigger celebration?"

He leaned against the wall next to her and let out a

long breath. "Do you remember Marlene Shaw, Kate's maternal grandmother?"

"*Maternal* hardly seems the word, if you'll forgive me," Maggie said.

He tried to smile but the heat of their previous moment wasn't quite behind him. "You know about her attempt to get custody of Kate."

Maggie nodded. "But she couldn't get custody away from you, you're Kate's father. I thought that was settled."

"Probably, but I want to be sure."

"I see," Maggie said slowly. "And it can't hurt for you to be a married man."

She was no fool. "No," he agreed. "It can only help."

She eyed him for a moment, then said, "So what's the problem?"

"You're not going to like it."

"I already hate it." She gave a dry laugh. "Now tell me."

He straightened his shoulders and looked her evenly in the eye. "Marlene has upped the ante. Now she's making threats."

"About what?"

"She doesn't believe that ours will be a real marriage."

"Well..."

"Okay, we both know what it is." *And after that kiss we both know what it could be.* "Marlene's calling it a calculated move."

Maggie said nothing but looked at him wide-eyed, as though she were trying not to laugh.

Alex let a breath out. "Okay, I see the irony of that, but my point remains. She's threatening to expose us."

"She can't. How would she know about our personal lives?"

"I don't know. But I don't want to give her any ammunition."

"Okay. So what does our ceremony have to do with that? What difference does it make whether it's in court or at St. Paul's?"

"She's equating location with commitment." He gave a wry laugh. "She's probably expecting a quick courthouse ceremony."

"Oh, I see. So we must prove her wrong at every turn."

"Right. So as for the wedding, I think it would be best if we had a little gathering here, in the house." He shoved his hands into his pockets. He felt like a high school kid on a first date. "On Saturday."

"Saturday." She let out a breath.

"Second thoughts?"

"No." Her response was reassuringly fast. "But…Saturday. That's five days away."

"Long enough to set up some sort of wedding, I hope."

Maggie looked panicked. "I'll have to start on the arrangements right away."

"No, you don't. I have people to take care of that sort of thing."

"I can't just let other people do it all."

"Why not?"

"It's *my* wedding." She hesitated and Alex noticed her cheeks flush again. "At least it's supposed to look like it. I have to keep up appearances."

"This will *appear* just right," Alex said, a little disgusted with his own concern for appearances.

"You just hire people for everything, don't you? If

you don't want to deal with it, then you just pay someone else to.''

He sighed. "Is there something wrong with that?''

"Do that enough, and you miss out on life completely. Before you know it, it's gone.''

"Are you finished?''

"For now.''

"Good. Now, I'll hire a planner to oversee everything. My secretary will have to phone invitations since
it's so close. If there's anyone in particular you'd like
to invite, give the names to Julia.''

"Do I have anything to do with this at all?'' Maggie
asked.

"Naturally. The wedding belongs to the bride. I'll
have an outline of the plans made for you. If you want
anything changed, talk with the wedding planner or my
secretary.''

Maggie looked at him then unexpectedly reached out
and touched his arm. "Why are you trying so hard to
distance yourself from your life?''

He paused, looking into her eyes, fighting a strong
compulsion to cover her hand with his own. "I don't
think I am.''

She withdrew her hand and his chance was lost.
"Shall we tell Kate now?''

"Sure.'' He drew an uncertain breath. "If you think
she's ready.''

"I'm not sure *any* of us are ready,'' Maggie said.
"But I think Kate, at least, will be very excited at the
idea of being in a wedding.''

Kate was sitting on her window seat, looking through
a *Madeline* book when Maggie and Alex opened the
door.

"Kate," Alex said.

She looked up quickly, dropping the book in her lap.

"I didn't mean to startle you." Why did he always feel like a St. Bernard with a kitten around her? He looked to Maggie, feeling strangely maladroit.

She was looking at him—no, *studying* him—with what appeared to be compassion. "Go ahead," she said encouragingly, with a smile he was sure was for Kate's benefit. When he didn't respond right away, she said to Kate, "Darling, Daddy and I have something awfully big to tell you." She looked back at Alex. "Go ahead."

Alex clasped his hands together in front of him. "Kate, Maggie and I have decided to get married."

Kate's eyes grew wide. "To each other?" She looked to Maggie for confirmation.

"Yes, darling," she said. "Isn't that terribly exciting?"

"I didn't even know you two *liked* each other!"

Alex and Maggie exchanged a nervous laugh. "We certainly do," Maggie said, a little too vehemently. "How would you like to get a beautiful dress and be a flower girl in the wedding?"

"Yes! When *is* the wedding?"

"Saturday," Alex answered. Then, following an impulse that he would normally have ignored, he went to his daughter and knelt in front of her. "Katie." He took her small hands between his fingertips. "I would never want to do anything that could hurt you in any way. You do know that don't you?"

Kate nodded.

"How do you feel about Maggie and I getting married? Is that okay by you?"

She nodded again. "I wished and wished this would happen. You can ask the stars outside my window."

She said this so earnestly that Alex had to suppress a smile. "You're a pretty powerful wisher then." He bent to kiss her on the cheek but she turned her head and bumped him in the nose. Swiftly he stood up. "I just wanted to be sure that this was all okay with you."

"It's great!" She smiled brightly, but the joy faded as fast as it came. Big eyes filled with trepidation turned to Maggie. "Are you going to be my mommy now?"

"We'll be buddies." Maggie sat down next to Kate on the floor. "Just like we are now."

"But if you're married to my daddy that makes you my mommy. It's like princesses who marry kings and then become queens," Kate explained patiently. Then she looked to Alex, with some concern in her eyes. "Does this mean I have to stop loving my first mommy?"

"No. You'll never stop loving her."

"You did."

He drew a tense breath, aware of Maggie's eyes upon him. "That was different. Mommy wasn't happy with me. I couldn't give her what she wanted."

"What did she want?"

What could he say? He couldn't explain that her mother wanted to be the Lady of the Manor but not a wife or mother. He couldn't tell her that her mother had wanted his money and a place in society—and had continually used Kate as a bargaining chip to get them and keep them after the divorce—but had found her pleasures with other men. Kate could never find that out. "Come on, this isn't about your mother and me. It's right for you to love your mother, and you always will. But you can love Maggie, too."

Would Maggie ever do the things that Sandra had? Would Maggie lie and cheat, then try to take him for all he was worth? Would Maggie slip off into the wood-work if he offered her enough money to disappear? After all, he'd been stupid enough to miss those qualities in Sandra at first.

Kate was still looking at Alex. "It's really okay for me to love Maggie?"

He looked at Maggie. Her eyes were unusually bright. She wasn't like Sandra, he was almost sure of it. "That's really okay."

"Are you two going to have a baby?"

Alex stopped breathing for a moment. He looked at Maggie, who looked as surprised as he felt. Her eyes were wide and a little panicked. Their gazes locked.

"Why would you ask something like that?" Maggie asked slowly, still holding Alex's gaze. Then she turned to Kate.

"Because married people have babies," Kate answered simply.

"Not always," Alex said sharply. He couldn't help wondering, if only momentarily, what a child of his and Maggie's would be like. Not that it was a possibility. Kate was his responsibility and he was going to take care of her the best way he knew how, but he knew he wasn't good father material.

How could he be? He'd had the lousiest teacher in the world.

"I want a sister," Kate was saying. "Or a brother. There's no one to play with."

Hesitantly Maggie turned her gaze to Kate. "You'll be starting first grade in the fall. Then you'll have tons of little friends to play with, almost all day long instead of just half a day like now."

Kate clicked her tongue against her teeth. "That's not the same."

Maggie smiled and gave Kate a squeeze. "But it's almost as good."

Kate crinkled her nose. "Why are you getting married then?"

"Wellll." Maggie swallowed and looked back to Alex. "For...several good reasons."

"You need a mother," Alex broke in. "Even without a brother or sister. Now Maggie will be like a mother."

"And she'll stay for a long, long time?"

"Right."

"Forever?"

Alex tensed. It had been a long time since he'd thought about *forever.*

Before he could answer, Maggie did. "I'll be here for as long as you need me," she said uneasily.

"Won't Daddy need you? Will you be here for as long as he needs you, too?"

Alex was surprised to find himself listening for her answer.

Maggie pursed her lips and considered. "Don't worry about that, Kate." Her green eyes lifted to him, then flitted back to Kate. "I think your daddy already has pretty much everything he needs."

Kate nodded but looked tentative.

"Is something wrong?" Maggie asked her.

"I need to go to the bathroom."

Maggie laughed. "Okay." She swept a hand toward the hallway and Kate went running.

When she was gone, Alex turned to Maggie. He clapped his hands together. "So. It's done."

Maggie stood. "Hardly. There's a lot to do suddenly."

"Make a list and give it to my secretary. She'll take care of anything you need."

Maggie gave a half smile. "Not very romantic, is it?"

He thought about her lips under his, that delicate tongue and the electric shock that surged through him when it touched his. "Maybe not. But it's sure going to *look* romantic," he said, watching her.

She nodded slowly and unconsciously moistened her lips as she had before. "I guess it will fool all the right people into thinking it's real."

Tension gathered in his groin. "That's what we want, isn't it? For it to look real? To fool people?"

"Yes." She looked away, suddenly fascinated by something on Kate's wall. "And we will. We'll fool them all."

The next afternoon Maggie was in the kitchen with Kate when Alex came in. He was wearing a dark blue pinstriped suit that picked up the vivid blue of his eyes. Maggie couldn't help the instant tripping of her heart.

"Is everything all right?" Alex asked, obviously detecting an odd look on her face.

"Fine." Maggie blinked hard, as if that would blot out the image. When she opened them, he was still there, leaning toward her and looking more devastatingly handsome than ever before. "You look nice," she managed to say, with what she hoped was casual ease. Suddenly aware of Kate at her side, she took her hand and said, "Doesn't Daddy look nice?"

"Yeah," Kate answered, but kept her eye on Maggie. "But you look funny."

Maggie's face grew warm. "I do?"

"That's just how you looked at those chocolate chip cookies you said we couldn't have before dinner," Kate said petulantly, and looked longingly at the cookie jar on the refrigerator. Then, with sudden hope she asked, "Did you change your mind? Can I have some now?"

Maggie's eyes met and locked with Alex's. "No."

"Aw, why not?"

"Yeah, why not?" Alex asked.

Still looking at him, she replied, "You can't always have things just because they look good."

"Although sometimes you can indulge yourself," Alex said, without looking away. "If you really want to. As long as you know what you're getting into."

Maggie swallowed. Her fingertips tingled with the memory of touching him and the longing to do it again. She wanted, for one crazy instant, to taste him and the heck with the cookies. "The price can be quite high, then before you know it, it's gone. And you have nothing to show for it."

"But if you *savor* it—" his voice became lower and a little raw "—it can last a long time." His eyes lingered on hers.

"You certainly make it sound tempting." Maggie was surprised at the waver in her voice. She gave as bright a smile as she could to belie her inner trembling, then looked away from the magnetic pull of his blue gaze. "We have an important day coming up. I don't want to blow it by eating a bunch of cookies and getting too fat for my dress."

He gave a small nod of concession. "Maybe another time, then."

She nodded mutely. She wondered if he knew what she was thinking at all, or if he was actually talking about cookies. He probably was.

"Right now I need to talk with you," Alex said, still searching her eyes. "Do you have a minute?"

Maggie turned to Kate, all too aware of the electricity

in the air. "Katie, why don't you go outside and play before dinner for a few minutes. Then you'll need to change your shirt." She pointed at a large chocolate milk stain across Kate's chest.

"Can we have the cookies after dinner?" Kate asked. "Pretty please?"

"Maybe. Run along now."

When she had gone out into the late afternoon sunshine, Maggie turned back to Alex. "What's up?"

"Now, I don't want you to panic."

Panic gripped her. Disastrous scenarios chased each other across her imagination: an accident, something had happened to her mother. "What is it? What's wrong?"

"Immigration called a little while ago."

"Immigration?" For a moment the word didn't register. She shook her head, uncomprehending. "Why?" The paperwork was done. Besides, the INS was too big an operation to call individuals on the phone, wasn't it?

"It's no big deal," Alex answered, though his tone suggested otherwise. "I'm sure it's standard operating procedure but...they want to have an interview with us. About our marriage."

Chapter Four

Maggie sucked in her breath. An Immigration interview was about the worst thing she could imagine sitting through. Her tapestry of emotions was difficult enough to hide from Alex when they were alone. Heaven only knew what sort of fool she would make of herself in a room with him *and* the INS. "They know. They know and they want to catch us in our lie."

"They don't know anything." Alex hesitated. "They just suspect." Then he smiled a devastatingly carefree smile.

"Suspect?" Maggie repeated, ignoring the smile as best she could. "But how? Why?" The answer was probably obvious but she couldn't think why they would look at her case so quickly.

His face grew more serious. "Marlene, undoubtedly. She probably called them the minute after I hung up with her."

"Is she so vindictive?"

His short burst of laughter was devoid of humor. "Oh, yeah."

Maggie sighed. "Oh, no."

He reached a hand to her shoulder, where it hovered for a moment before he gave a single awkward pat. "But don't worry about it, it'll be fine. After all, we *have* been living together for six months."

"But we don't know anything about each other!"

His reply was pointed. "I think we know enough."

Maggie felt as if she'd been struck. Without knowing anything, he knew *enough* about her. She hadn't raised an iota of curiosity in him. Over the months, she'd been watching him, fighting her romantic feelings for him even as she knew that the one thing she could never live with—the fact that his career came before all else—would probably never change. Yet there was so much there, so much that touched her heart when she took just a moment to look. Moments of hastily masked vulnerability in him, produced a hollow ache in her heart every time. Moments when she'd been sure he was about to reveal something more of himself filled her with hope but he always retreated at the last moment, always returned to the hard shell of defenses that protected him: work, conferences, business trips.

At first she thought she could reach him, that it would only be a matter of time before she could coax him out of his shell, the way she had Kate. But it hadn't happened and by now her nerves were worn from the number of times she'd stood before him, willing him with all the power of her being to open up, only to be disappointed.

In that time she'd learned to read almost all of his moods. When he was anxious or worried, he ran his hands through his hair but he never noticed the rumpled effect. Maggie found the look charming. When he was angry, his brow grew straight and his eyes dark. He spoke brusquely, in single syllables. When he was happy...well, she'd been looking for happy but so far she'd never really seen it. He kept his deepest emotions in tight check. It would probably never change.

But with all that she knew, she really knew nothing. They knew nothing about each other.

And for him that was enough.

"What's wrong?" Alex asked, shaking her out of her thoughts.

She couldn't meet his eyes. "Nothing. I—*I* just don't feel we know enough. To satisfy the INS, I mean."

"Really?" He looked surprised. "What do you want to know?" Then, with an apparent flash of perception, he added, "What do you want me to know?"

She felt her face grow warm. "I don't know. What sort of questions will they ask?"

"Basic stuff, more than likely. If Marlene has dropped a hint that our marriage might be a sham, they'll probably ask us details about each other. Where you went to school, the name of your village in England, that sort of thing."

"Then I should probably tell you those things."

"I already know quite a bit." She knew her expression was stunned, and he smiled. "You grew up in Highgate, then moved to Newhaven with your mother after your father's death. You went to a boarding school briefly, then attended comprehensive in Newhaven. You did fairly well on your O levels and A levels, then came here to the Montessori Institute, which is when we met."

Maggie felt a chill creep down the back of her neck. "How do you know all of that?"

"It's basic information, Maggie. Easily found in a background check."

"You did a *background check* on me?"

"*I* didn't." Relief cooled her insides until he added, "I had a detective do it." Shock burned in her gut until he added, "I do that with all my employees."

The emotion vanished, leaving a black hole. "I see," she said.

"I hope you don't find that insulting."

She thought about it for a moment, then said, "From your point of view, I'm sure it makes good sense. I can't say I'm really comfortable with it, though. What else do you know?"

"Nothing very personal," he answered. "Just that you're here now and your mother remains in New-haven."

Her stomach twisted as she thought of her mother in her tiny tenement in Newhaven. Her mother, who had once been so proud and who now, because of crippling arthritis, struggled for a modest life-style with the help of the British government and Maggie. Did Alex know about those checks she sent each week? Was that pity she saw in his eyes? "Well," Maggie said a little awkwardly, "you seem to know an awful lot about me but I know very little about you."

"I'm not all that interesting."

"I doubt the INS would agree." At any rate she, herself, didn't agree. "I could tell them the name of your company, or the colors of your cars, but if they asked me what you like to eat, I don't think I could answer."

"Well." He gave a shrug. "I'm your basic meat and potatoes kind of guy. Nothing special. I'll eat pretty

much everything.'' He hesitated. ''Except mushrooms.
I hate mushrooms.''

''*Hate* them?''

''*Hate* them.''

Maggie laughed. It was just about the most passionate
thing he'd ever said to her. ''I do, too.''

A moment of silence passed.

''How do you feel about pizza?'' Alex asked.

''Ah.'' She smiled. It wasn't a particularly deep conversation but it was a start. ''I love pizza. Absolutely
adore it.''

''You know,'' he said, smiling. ''There's a place
downtown that makes the best pizza I've ever had,
Faccia Luna. It's cooked in a wood-burning oven.
We—'' He stopped and shrugged. ''You really should
try it sometime.''

Maggie's heart soared and crashed. She knew their
moment was over and no matter what she said, she
couldn't get it back. She'd tried before, many times.

She held a heavy sigh in check. Better to just go
along as if she hadn't any higher hopes for their relationship than he did.

''I'll keep it in mind,'' she said, picking up a paper-
weight and concentrating on it. ''Thanks for the suggestion.''

''Maggie,'' he began. His voice was hushed.

Her breath caught in her throat. ''Yes?''

He shoved his hands into his pockets. ''Maybe…you
have a point. About us getting to know each other a
little better. Not that I want to bore you with a lot of
personal detail,'' he quickly amended. ''But a little
background would probably be helpful.''

She was practically on her toes waiting for his next
words. ''I think it would.''

Then he looked at his watch and her heart sank.

"I wish we could sit down now but I have a meeting downtown in an hour and then a business dinner," he said. "But maybe we could get—"

Before he could finish, Kate came bursting through the back door. "Quick! You have to come quick!" she cried. Her face was flushed, her eyes wide and panicked.

Alex didn't hesitate. In one second he was at Kate's side. "What's wrong?" He laid a hand on her shoulder.

She wriggled out from under his grasp. "You have to see. Come quick!" She dashed out the door with Alex close behind.

Maggie hung back for a moment, torn between desire to let them go and be together without her and the compulsion to help when called. It was her help instinct that won out and she hurried out to the spot under a large oak tree, where Alex and Kate stood.

"We *have* to do something!" Kate was crying.

Alex looked nonplussed. "We can't interfere. Nature has its own way of taking care of things."

"What's going on?" Maggie asked, stepping up next to Alex. The scent of his aftershave mingled with the late spring blossoms and Maggie had to work to resist the urge to step even closer to him. It was an urge she had become used to squelching.

He turned blue eyes on her and screwed up his brow. "A baby bird has fallen out of its nest." He gestured toward the ground several feet away.

Kate bent down and reached a finger toward the peeping bird. "We have to save it."

"Kate!" Alex's shout startled her and she looked at him like a frightened puppy. He stepped over and squatted beside her, laying an awkward hand on her back.

"I'm sorry, I didn't mean to scare you. But maybe we should leave it there where its mother can find it."

Kate didn't look at him. "Its mother isn't coming back," she said quietly, staring at the bird.

Alex gave a laugh. "Of course its mother will come back. She'll notice one of her babies is gone and come looking for it. Now, come on, let's go in."

Maggie looked at the little bird, then at Kate, who stared at it with a strange intensity. Then Maggie turned her gaze to Alex and saw him watching Kate, too. But he had a frown where she would have liked to have seen compassion. Those wonderful features of his were capable of such strange detachment, and Maggie saw that now.

"We can't just leave it here," Kate argued, turning liquid eyes to Maggie. "Tell him, Maggie."

"I'm not sure what to do," Maggie said. "There's an old wives' tale that if you touch them their mothers won't take them back—"

"Its mother *isn't* coming back," Kate said again, her small voice firm. "I *know* she isn't."

A bird chirped overhead and they all looked up.

"There," Alex said with satisfaction. "That must be her now. Let's get out of the way, Kate, so they can get back together."

"I'm not going," Kate said, through gritted teeth. Her determination was fierce, but she didn't look at either Maggie or Alex. Maggie recognized that Kate was afraid to cross her father even as she did so.

"Kate." This time Alex's voice was harder. "Come on." He looked at his watch.

Maggie's stomach tightened. The bird overhead flew away.

Kate stood up and balled her small hands into fists.

"You don't understand!" she cried. "You don't even care!"

"How can you say I don't care?" Alex asked. "You know I care about you."

"You don't care about anything but your dumb old work." Her voice grew shrill and tears poured from her eyes. "Even if someone dies, you don't care. You don't care about anything!"

Alex looked as if he'd been sucker-punched in the gut. "No one's going to die."

"You don't know that!"

"Kate," he said stiffly, and reached a hand out toward her. "Let's go. You have to get ready for dinner anyway."

She reeled backward. "No!"

Maggie, who had been firmly holding her tongue, closed her eyes and prayed silently for a miracle. This was important—this could be the defining moment of Alex and Kate's relationship. She couldn't interfere unless it looked like it was hopeless.

Alex looked to her for a moment, then back at Kate. "Come in now," he said, more firmly.

"No, no, no, no!" Kate cried, stomping her foot. "I won't go. You can't make me."

Maggie noticed Alex flinch. For a moment he was silent, then he took a long breath and said, "Kate, you can't start these tantrums again."

This was what he considered a tantrum? He'd said he'd lost other nannies because Kate threw temper tantrums. What sort of nannies had he hired before that left over such typical child behavior? Naughty behavior, to be sure, but still typical. It was certainly nothing to get overly alarmed about.

Once again, Alex looked at Maggie, this time imploringly. Maggie said nothing. But she gave him the smallest nod, what she hoped was a sign of encouragement. With a sigh, and narrowed eyes, he shook his head at her, then went to Kate and reached for her hand. She pulled her arm back and he caught her instead by the wrist. His grasp remained there. "The mother is never going to come back with us standing here, let's go."

"The cats will get it," Kate wailed.

"What cats?"

"The ones next door. They have *tons* of them."

"No cats are going to get over here." He pulled gently on her wrist. "Let's *go*."

Kate planted her feet and hung back. It was almost comical, the tug-of-war between the wiry little girl and the powerfully built man. Alex had to be at least six foot one, and Kate was barely over three feet. If it hadn't been so excruciating to watch them act out the roles both were so ill prepared for, Maggie would have found the whole thing terribly amusing.

But instead it was very difficult.

"I won't go without the birdie!" Kate cried. "We can't let it die!"

He pulled her gently. "It's not going to die."

She tried to wrench her arm free, then twisted around to face the bird. "I won't leave it there! No!"

"The bird's not going to die," Alex said through clenched teeth. "I told you its mother will come for it." He gave a half shrug and let go of her wrist. "That's what mothers do."

"No, they don't," Kate said fiercely, putting her hands behind her back. "The mother's not coming back."

Maggie's heart constricted. *No, they don't.* She bit

her lip and tried to keep sudden tears from burning her eyes. How could she have taken so long to get it? *The mother's not coming back.* She tried to swallow but her throat was tight. The urge to take Kate in her arms was overwhelming, but she couldn't. It was up to Alex. She looked at him but saw no sign that he recognized the cause of Kate's intense anxiety.

"Forget about the bird, it will be okay," Alex barked. "We're going in. Stop acting like a brat."

"I hate you!" Kate cried.

"Kate!" Alex's expression was pained but not surprised.

Tears flowed freely down her cheeks now. "I *do*, I *hate* you! I wish I'd never come to this place! If you send me away again I won't care! I *want* to go!" She ran, sobbing, back to the spot where the baby bird was still peeping.

Alex muttered an oath.

"Alex," Maggie said quietly.

He turned and looked at her. "So *now* you've decided to speak?" His sarcasm was softened by the deep concern in his eyes.

Maggie felt her face grow warm, wanting to comfort him as well as Kate. "Kate's worried that the baby bird's mother won't come for it."

"I know, she said that. I told her it will."

Maggie gave a single shake of her head, widened her eyes and lowered her chin along with her voice. "She's *upset* because she thinks the baby's *mother* is *not coming back.* And on top of that she's afraid you're going to send her away for saying so. Just like she was sent away before, from *her mother's* house to *yours.*"

Finally the light dawned in his eyes. Maggie heard his sharp intake of breath as he raked a hand through his hair. After a moment, he turned back to Kate. "Honey," he said, gently. He walked over to her slowly and knelt a couple of feet away. "Are you worried that bird's mommy is going to leave it because you feel like your mommy left you?"

"Sh-sh-she did," Kate stuttered through tears.

Alex shook his head and Maggie could have sworn she saw his eyes grow bright. In a blink they looked normal again. "No, sweetheart, she didn't. We talked about this, she didn't want to leave you."

"But she did leave." Kate looked back at the pathetic creature on the ground. "She's gone. And she's not coming back. It's the same with the bird. Its mother is *gone*."

"Even if that's true, someone else will love and take care of the baby." He hesitated. "In fact, maybe the daddy bird will come get the baby and be as happy to have it come live with him as I was to have you come live with me."

Kate sniffled. "You had to take me."

"I *wanted* to take you. I would have been happy if your mother had never taken you away in the first place."

"Really?" Kate was dubious.

"Really. Did you know this was your first home?"

"No, it wasn't." But she sounded interested.

"Yes. When you were first born we brought you home and put you into a white crib in the same room you have now..." His voice wavered. He stopped and swallowed.

For the second time, Maggie thought she saw tears glistening in his eyes, then nothing.

Alex ran his hand across Kate's hair. "You know, maybe you're right about that little bird after all. I've heard of people taking them in and feeding them some kind of mush through an eyedropper until they're strong enough to fly away.''

Kate turned to him and blinked her wide, wet eyes. ''Could we?'' She sniffed. ''Can I take care of the bird until it can fly?''

Alex looked at Maggie. ''Any idea how to do this? What about that old wives' tale about not touching the bird?''

Maggie smiled. ''What do old wives know? I think there's an old shoebox we could use as a sort of nest. Maybe we could put a little grass or straw down. Actually, I do think I've heard that's the thing to do.''

''What do we feed it?'' Kate asked Alex.

''Feed it,'' he repeated. ''Mmm. Twinkies?''

Kate giggled, reluctantly. ''No.''

''Hamburgers?''

''No.''

''Hmm.'' He frowned. ''Maybe we should call the animal shelter and ask them.''

''Do you know their number?''

He smiled. ''We'll find it.'' He stood up and reached down for Kate's hand to help her up.

''I'm going to get the bird,'' Kate said, putting her hands out.

''Better let me.'' Alex took his jacket off and gently reached down for the baby bird. Maggie watched his large, strong hands pick the bird up with tremendous care. Serious concern etched his even features. With no hint of distaste on his face, he placed the bird on the expensive satiny lining of his jacket to carry it inside. Maggie smiled to herself. The lowered expression he wore only emphasized the sensual curve of his lips and his straight brow. For just a moment his eyes flitted to hers and the corner of his mouth curved up fractionally.

Maggie's breath left her.

Kate rushed ahead toward the house, declaring that she was going to open the door for "Daddy and Beaky." Alex watched her go, then started to follow.

"Stop looking so smug," he said under his breath as he passed Maggie. There was a smile in his eyes, if not on his lips. "I would've caught on. In another couple of years."

"I'd say you did pretty well," Maggie said. "Better than a lot of parents out there." She thought of her own father and realized with a start that she could barely recall the details of his face. She wondered if she ever could—he'd been gone more than he'd ever been around. In a soft voice she finished. "A lot of parents wouldn't even have bothered to try. They consider their children mere inconveniences. If they consider them at all."

Alex's expression turned to stone. "Don't praise me for not being a jerk. I don't deserve it."

The walls were up again. Maggie had seen the transformation too many times not to recognize it. With a heavy heart she said, "I just hope you'll keep trying. Don't ever give up on her—she needs you. She loves you."

"I don't know about *that*. You heard her say she hates me. She said she wishes she'd never come here. I know she was upset, but that sort of comment doesn't come out of the blue."

Maggie searched his eyes but didn't understand the detachment she saw there. "It came from worrying about the bird," she said. "She didn't mean any of it."

"It came—" he corrected lowly "—from having a

lousy father." There was certainty in his voice, along with a disturbing acceptance.

"You sound pretty sure about that."

He shrugged. "Oh, I have no illusions about it. Lousy fathering is hereditary in my family." He didn't smile.

"That's a good old cop-out," Maggie said, fighting back anger.

"It's no cop-out."

She clicked her tongue against her teeth. "If there's one thing I recognize, it's a cop-out." *I can't do any more for the child. We haven't the time to coddle her. Either she learns to act like a proper young lady on her own, or she goes to boarding school to do it. I've far too much to do, to worry about an unruly child.* Maggie closed her eyes for a long moment pushing the unwanted memory aside, then opened them and straightened her back. "If you say it's hereditary, then you're saying it's beyond your control."

"Sometimes it seems to be."

"Oh, come off it. Nothing you do is beyond your control." She raised her chin. "If you really want to change things, you can. Or you can stay as emotionally distant as you want, hire people to take care of everything for Kate and spend a moment with her each week when you have the time, but *don't* say it's beyond your control. That's a lie."

Alex stopped and looked at her so icily she almost feared for the tiny life he held in his hands. "When you have children of your own, *then* you can come tell me all the things I'm doing wrong and how to correct them. Until then—" he put the coat and bird into her hands "—maybe you'd better stick to your job."

He walked back to the house, leaving her there with the bundle in her hands. For long seconds she stood there, watching his back. Finally, when he'd disappeared into the house, she willed the tears to come but they wouldn't. She just felt empty. Having a family of her own was one of the most important things she could imagine. Countless times she'd thought to herself if she had a child and a home that was permanent she could face anything else in the world with courage. If she had a child like Kate she would never take her for granted. And if she had a husband like Alex...

Well, she was about to have that, but it was a mockery. The setup would be a sham and Alex had just reminded her of that in no uncertain terms. She had a function to perform and that function was to work her way into obsolescence, to help take care of Kate so that Kate would grow secure enough—or out of the house enough—to do without her care.

Only then would Alex be satisfied with Maggie Weller.

By the time he got to his office, Alex was shaking. He paced back and forth across the floor, trying to calm his humming nerves. Who did Maggie think she was? Why couldn't she ever just let him do things his own way? Why couldn't she accept the fact that he was never going to be Ward Cleaver? Why the hell didn't she realize that was why he'd hired *her?* Did she think men like Ward Cleaver and whatever Fred Mac-Murray's character was on "My Three Sons" needed to hire nannies for their kids?

Of course not.

But men like Alex did. They found warm, caring people like Maggie to make up for their own shortcomings, not to point them out. That is, if they cared enough. The rest of them just let their kids fend for themselves. Or, worse, used them as whipping boys for their own problems.

When they weren't drowning those problems in alcohol.

Alex stopped and took several deep breaths. Maggie had a lot of power to make him feel rotten. He couldn't quite figure out why. He wanted to think it was because Maggie was so much more important to Kate than he was, but that didn't quite answer it. After all, Maggie was doing her job and doing it well.

It was the fact that she kept trying to get him to do more that bothered him. And he was going to *marry* her! He started pacing again. She would be relentless in her suggestions for improving his parenting. At least it was only for three months. At the end of the summer she would move into her own place and leave him some peace.

He laughed. Peace! Fat chance of that. He hadn't known peace in years. Maybe he never had.

But he'd come closer in the past five months with Maggie than he had ever come before. If only he could stop her from constantly criticizing his parenting.

He shook his head and went to the dry bar. He couldn't stop her from criticizing his parenting, he thought as he poured himself a neat bourbon. She was right about him. And she was an expert on childrens' needs. That's what he'd hired her for. He picked up the glass and looked at the pungent liquid within.

It wasn't just Maggie, it was women.

All women.

He just couldn't deal with women in his life. Sandra had proven that. True, Maggie was no Sandra, but they both shared the most damnable quality of their sex— the power to turn Alex inside out. The power to show him just how inadequate he was, Sandra by feeding him lies and Maggie by telling him the truth. It all amounted to the same thing.

His grip tightened on the glass. He looked down at his hand. But it wasn't his hand, it was his father's. The same square palm, the same long fingers wrapped around the same glass of liquid courage. *His father's hands. His father's drink.*

He dropped the glass. It shattered into a thousand pieces at his feet. For a long moment he just stood there, looking at the mess. Then he took a slow step away from it, wishing he could step so easily away from his past.

His father may have wished the same thing. Lord knew he'd walked away from his family enough. Turned his back on Alex and his mother.

Was Alex doing that now?

He walked to his desk and sat down heavily. Maybe he was. Most people followed in their fathers' footsteps, whether they intended to or not. But Maggie was right—it wasn't beyond his own control. Saying it *was* only a cop-out. And blaming Maggie for his discomfort with the truth was also a cop-out. He just didn't know if he could change.

Though she would never stop trying to get him to.

He looked at the desk calendar and let out a heavy breath. Two days. In two days he would be married again. Granted, it was only in name, but still…Maggie was going to be his wife. She was going to be living in this house the same way she had been for the last five months, but she was going to be his *wife*.

A tremor ran through him and he picked up a pen. Three months. His heart thudded dully in his chest. It wasn't very long. He traced a line through the days on his desk blotter until the end of the third month. September fourth. He drew in a wavering breath. For all intents and purposes, Maggie was only going to be his wife until September fourth. Then it would be over. For all intents and purposes.

He circled the date and sat back with a sigh.

Chapter Five

The night before the wedding, Alex and Maggie arranged to meet on the terrace after dinner to discuss any last-minute details. And to get their story straight in case they should be questioned by Marlene or anyone else. She met him outside at seven, as the sun was sinking in the sky.

"How are you feeling?" he asked her, a little awkwardly. It sounded like code for something else, as if they were both working on some top secret project. *How are you feeling?* actually meant *Have you changed your mind?*

"I'm fine," she answered, which really meant *I'm terrified.* She cocked her head. "How are *you* feeling?"

"Oh, fine, fine." He shoved his hands into his back pockets and looked at the ground. The deep amber light of sunset shone on his glossy dark hair, making it look touched with red. Maggie studied the way it curled, and the even cut that met his collar. She remembered touching it the day they'd kissed in the hall, how soft and thick it was.

He looked up. The light gleamed on his skin and in his eyes, making the blue look very clear. The cliché of comparing eyes to jewels had always annoyed Maggie, but suddenly *sapphire* struck her as the only description of that color.

"Are you hungry?" he asked.

She was surprised that it took her an instant to find her voice. "Not very," she finally managed to say. "A bit tired, though. I'm about ready for bed."

He raked his fingers through his hair. "Yeah, me too."

Their eyes met for an instant, then both looked away.

"This is some sunset," Maggie said, turning to face it.

He came up behind her. "*Red sky at night, sailor's delight*...tomorrow should be beautiful."

Maggie stepped back and accidentally knocked into him. His hands instantly grasped her shoulders. She turned to face him and his hands dropped back to his sides. They stood facing each other.

"Hopefully it won't be too hot," Maggie said, a little breathlessly. He was so close she could have wrapped her arms around him without taking a step forward.

He looked at her and drew in a breath.

"Is there any such thing as 'too hot'?"

"I...I don't know."

The sun cast a deep golden glow on her skin, and her eyes shone in the shimmering light. "After the cold spring we had, I don't think it could get too hot for me," Alex said softly, stepping toward her.

"It was cold. For so long." She tilted her chin up toward him. Her lips were slightly parted.

He couldn't stand it any longer. He took a step away but heat still pulsed through his body. "I had a call from Marlene today. She's responsible for our interview with the INS. Not that that's a surprise. But she's using her considerable weight to urge a thorough investigation of our marriage."

"What does that mean?"

"It means she has entirely too much time on her hands."

She lowered her lashes for a moment, then looked directly into Alex's eyes. The evening sun seemed to shine right through her eyes, making them a brilliant green. "But what does it mean for us?" she asked.

Us. He liked the way she said that. But then, he'd always liked English accents. "It means we have to really know our stuff." His eyes roamed over her face. "We have to know each other inside and out."

She swallowed. When she spoke, it was little more than a whisper. "I'm willing to study."

His heart began to pound. Damn this physical reaction he had around Maggie! Why couldn't she have been hideous, with the personality of a doormat, or of Anna Christianson? "We're talking a lot of studying, and fast."

"We have all night."

He couldn't help it. He took a step toward her. "You don't mind burning the midnight oil?" He reached out and touched her cheek.

He saw her draw a long breath. "I don't mind heating it…"

"Maggie." Impulsively he lowered his mouth onto hers. Her taste was just as he'd remembered it, and already comfortably familiar. Intoxicating, even. Common sense knocked at the door of his conscience but he ignored it. This was too good to resist.

Her arms snaked around him, and pulled him closer to her. Every warning signal in his mind went off, but he ignored them all. Maggie's fingernails, ran gently across his shoulders, and he groaned and deepened the kiss. He flattened his hand on the small of her back and pulled her toward him.

Then she pulled back. "This is wrong."

"No," he said, pulling her to him. "It's right. We're almost married." He lowered his mouth onto hers again, and she responded eagerly for just a moment, then pulled away again.

"No," she said firmly. She took another step backward, chest heaving. "That's just it. We'll always be *almost married.* At least for the summer. After that it will only be a technicality for just over two and a half years before we're married at all. None of this has anything to do with why we're getting married and I really feel like we shouldn't get it all mixed up."

She was right, his brain said. But he kissed her again anyway, and she responded with as much hunger as he felt. Their tongues touched, then shied away, then touched again, this time with more confidence. She ran her hands up his back and buried them in his hair. He pulled her closer. His heart pounded. He wanted her. He needed her.

Needed her? Alex didn't need anyone. He *couldn't* need anyone.

He pulled back abruptly. "I'm sorry." He looked for more words but none came to him.

Maggie's teeth sank into her upper lip and she looked down for a moment before returning her gaze to him. She looked shaken.

"I shouldn't have..." He shrugged. "I won't do that again." Why did he keep having to remind himself that this was business? He dropped his hands to his sides, then sighed and looked at the sunset. "We have an agreement." He shook his head. "Which reminds me, I have something for you."

"Something for me?"

He slipped a black velvet box out of his pocket. "It's this."

Her face fell. He could see her swallow convulsively. "That's for me?"

Good Lord, she looked horrified. That wasn't exactly the reaction he'd anticipated. "I was planning to give it to the first woman I saw out here tonight," he said with a humorless laugh. "That's you." He tossed her the box.

She caught it. "What's inside?"

"Open it."

She gave him a skeptical look and creaked the box open. "Alex." She gave a sharp intake of breath and took the sparkling ring out of the box. "What's this for?"

"It's an engagement ring," he answered.

"It's beautiful." She admired it for a few seconds, then closed the box. "But I can't accept it."

"It's just a ring." He shifted uncomfortably as a silence picked up and lengthened between them. "At least try it on."

She shook her head. "It's far too personal. I hate to keep harping on this, but if you remember our deal—"

"I remember our deal," Alex grumbled. "But take the damn ring because otherwise people will notice that you *don't* have one."

"Oh." She touched a hand to her cheek. "I hadn't thought of that."

"Fortunately I had."

She slipped the ring onto her finger.

Watching her, he said, "Normally a ring like that would be accompanied by a mushy proposal. At least I spared you that, huh?"

To his surprise, her lower lip trembled and she sank her teeth into it. Then her eyes grew bright. "This is difficult," she said.

"I wish it weren't."

She took her hand and swiped at a tear that rolled down her cheek. "I'm sorry. I don't mean to be over-emotional. It's probably just the—" she looked around "—it's probably just the night air." She shrugged, clearly realizing how inadequate the excuse was. "I'm tired. We have a bit more time—maybe we can prepare for the INS later."

Alex stepped back. "Of course." He turned his eyes away. "Let's just call it a night. Tomorrow is going to be a long day."

What a fool she'd made of herself. Practically breaking down and crying when he gave her the ring, as if it were an actual token of affection, rather than a show-piece to make people believe their story on Saturday.

Her romantic impulses toward him were crazy. He wasn't in this for a real marriage with her, and she knew it. He had much more important things to work out with Kate. Maggie should encourage that, not get in the way of it by making emotional demands that he couldn't understand, much less fulfill.

Alex Harrison **had** a limited reserve of both time and

emotion. It would be unconscionable of her to take any away from Kate for herself.

She looked at her left hand, at the exquisite diamond and emerald ring he'd given her. It fit perfectly. Men as smooth as Alex had a sense about that sort of thing, she supposed.

The glittering spread in her tear-filled eye. It was a beautiful ring, no matter what. She sighed. It was troubling. Alex was a man she could really care about. God forbid, she could probably fall in love with him, given half a chance.

And she wore his ring. It seemed like the perfect arrangement.

Yet she wasn't really engaged. Not in the spiritual sense that she'd always dreamed about. She was just wearing jewelry.

With a quick jerk, she took the ring off and put it away.

It was Saturday. Maggie's wedding day. She pulled the covers up to her chin and rolled over in bed. This couldn't be happening. A little more than a week ago she'd had no inkling that this was to come and now here it was.

She rolled over again and looked at the clock. It was half past eight. Her eyes flitted to the wedding dress, hanging in a plastic cover on her closet door. Her heart tripped, then sank. She had to keep perspective on this. It was an arrangement, she reminded herself yet again. Alex wasn't *really* going to be her husband.

She thought of the lacy peignoir her friend Ruth had given her as a wedding present. Ruth, a friend from the Montessori Institute, was to be Maggie's maid of honor today. True romantic that she was, she refused to believe that the marriage wasn't going to be a love match and had insisted on giving Maggie the lingerie.

Well, despite Ruth's romantic hopes, Maggie wouldn't be needing it. Might as well donate it to a charity for people with healthy love lives.

She creaked out of bed and went to the shower. When she came out fifteen minutes later, Ruth was waiting for her in her room, holding a blue dress on a hanger and her purse.

"Ready or not," Ruth sang.

"Here I come," Maggie finished. She took the dress off the hook and peeled back the plastic cover. "You don't think cream coloring is too...white, do you?"

"Too *white*? From what I understand blinding white would be appropriate for you two." She clicked her tongue against her teeth. "But the dress is gorgeous." Ruth tossed her purse onto the bed. "Let's see it on you."

Maggie took the dress down. She changed quickly then turned to Ruth, who was slipping her stockings on.

"Maggie, Alex is going to drop dead when he sees you in that."

A vein throbbed in Maggie's forehead. "I seriously doubt it."

"So you're still pretending, eh?"

"Pretending?"

"Yes. Pretending you're not in love with him."

"Shh! No one can hear that this is a fake." She swallowed. "Anyway, I'm *not* in love with him," she whispered.

"You are and, what's more, I think you have been ever since you started working for him."

Maggie swallowed convulsively and wondered if

Alex thought he saw the same thing. "You have a rich imagination."

Ruth ignored that. "What I don't get is why you refuse to admit it. Because you don't think he's in love with you?"

"I *know* he's *not* in love with me. I am an acquisition. And a temporary acquisition at that."

Ruth snorted and pulled her dress off the hanger. "Even if that's true, don't forget you've got three years to change it."

Maggie turned away and retrieved her hairbrush, anything to keep from having to look her friend in the eye. "I'm only here for three months."

"Okay, three months to change it. It's not a long time, but if you put your mind to it—"

"It's not going to happen, Ruth. And I don't want to talk about it anymore."

"Okay, okay. I can see you've made up your mind about things," Ruth said. "Consider the subject dropped." She brushed some lint off her shoulder. "The kitchen help has arrived. I saw them when I came in. I told them to start setting up outside."

"Good." Maggie took a deep breath. Then she looked at Ruth in the mirror behind her. "I'm sorry. I didn't mean to sound snappish before. This is...strange. I thought I could go through with it and not be all wrapped up emotionally but..." Her voice trailed off.

Ruth walked up behind her and put a hand on Maggie's shoulder. "Are you okay?"

Maggie turned her gaze to her reflection. "It's really going to happen."

Ruth smiled. "Yes, it's really going to happen. And it's going to be great. You mark my words."

* * *

Maggie stopped off in Kate's room on the way downstairs and sent Ruth ahead to check on the setting up. Kate was playing quietly with her dolls. A frothy pink dress lay on her bed, with a pair of lime green tights.

"What are you doing, Kate?"

Kate looked up and smiled. "Daddy said I should wait for you to help me get dressed. He didn't think my stockings would look good."

Maggie suppressed a smile. "We bought white tights to go with that dress. Where are they?"

"In the drawer. They're just not very *colorful.*"

"Today, I think we should go with the white. That will be just like what I'm wearing, see?" Maggie pointed her toe toward Kate. "We'll be almost like twins."

This brightened the child's face considerably. "Okay!" She jumped up and started changing her clothes.

Maggie sat down on the edge of the bed to wait. Every movement Kate made exuded excitement in a broad way. "Today are you going to have the same last name as me?" Kate asked, shrugging the dress over her head.

Maggie reached out and zipped the back for her. "Yes, come to think of it, I will." Good Lord, she hadn't even thought about that before. She was going to be Maggie Harrison today. Maggie Weller was going to fade into the past, or into a deep sleep, like Snow White.

"Now everyone will know you're married to my father, just by your name." She plunked down on the bed and thrust her feet at Maggie, for her to buckle her shoes.

Maggie laughed and buckled them. "That's right."

There was a knock at the door, then it swung open slowly. "Can I come in?" Alex asked.

"Yes." Maggie resented the instant thump of her heart.

It only got worse.

He stepped in, wearing a well-fitted dark gray suit. His dark hair was smoothed back and in place—no careless running of his hands through it today. In fact, he displayed none of the symptoms Maggie was feeling: shaking hands, pale skin, uncertain movements. He looked instead to be in absolute command of himself and his surroundings.

Kate stepped onto the floor and spun around. "How do I look?" she asked.

Alex held out his arms to Kate. "You are going to be the second prettiest girl there."

She hurled herself into his embrace. "You mean after Maggie?" she asked. "Doesn't Maggie look *beautiful?*"

Alex's eyes met Maggie's and held. "Yes. She's beautiful." He released Kate but not Maggie's gaze. "Beautiful."

There was another knock at the door and Ruth poked her head around the corner. "Sorry, Maggie, but there's a problem with the champagne. Did you know there's only one case of it?"

Maggie turned to her, disappointed that she had interrupted the moment. "There's more in the cellar," she said. "Mike will bring it up if we need it."

"Thanks." Ruth disappeared.

Maggie turned back to Alex but Kate held a bow in front of her eyes. "Can you put this in my hair?"

Maggie took the bow and silently secured it in Kate's hair, feeling Alex's eyes on her the entire time.

"There," she said when she finished. "All through. Now let's go downstairs and see if Ruth found Mike."

"Can I have a minute?" Alex said to Maggie. His blue eyes were warmer than she'd ever seen them. Or maybe it was she who was more compelled by them than ever before. He smiled. "This may be the last chance we get at peace today."

Maggie gave Kate a playful swat on the behind. "Run along, child. You're going to have to help Ruth without me for the moment. Tell her I'll be right down."

When Kate was gone, she turned back to Alex. "What's on your mind?"

He cleared his throat. "This isn't easy. I thought it would be easier but..."

Maggie felt her heart start to pound, but somehow managed to stand still. "Is there a problem?"

"I hope not." He shrugged. "I wanted to make sure you know what you're doing."

There was another knock at the door.

"Go away," Alex called.

Maggie shot him a look. "Yes?" she said.

The maid, Bess, opened the door timidly. "Telephone for Mr. Harrison."

"Take a message," he said through gritted teeth. He turned back to Maggie.

She frowned. "What brought all of this up? About me knowing what I'm doing, I mean."

"It's been a lot of things, lately. I'm just worried we're not on the same wavelength about our relationship."

She shook her head. "Our agreement—"

"I know, I know, the agreement. I'm already sick of the damned agreement."

"It's just good business," she reminded him in his own words. "It helps everyone remember their objectives."

"That's true. But sometimes circumstances change."

"So what's different now?"

He ran a hand through his hair. "I guess you could say that I, I…"

Was he asking what she thought he was asking? She tilted her head and studied him. It would have been so easy to agree to more if he wanted it. The man was gorgeous. She would love to indulge the hedonistic possibilities, but if she did it would be like acknowledging to the world that she wasn't worth any more than that.

And she *was*. She was worth a lot more than that, she reminded herself.

"You drew the parameters very specifically in our contract and I agreed to them," she said. "We're in this for the good it will do Kate. Nothing has changed as far as that's concerned."

"Things *have* changed. That's what I've been trying to tell you. I'm not sure I can ignore that."

"Alex!" This time it was Alex's secretary Julia who appeared. "You have *got* to get the phone. The tent isn't here and they say it can't get here before four."

"Take care of it," he growled. "I'm busy."

"But—"

"Forget the tent, just leave us alone."

"Sorry," Julia said, backing out.

He turned back to Maggie. "As I was saying—"

She held up her hands. While the temptation to sleep with him was strong, she was not going to allow herself to add sex to their relationship. It could only hurt her in the end. "I think I know what you were saying, but

I think it's best if we just keep our understanding the way it is. Can you?''

"Yes. My fears were only that, well, maybe staying the whole summer is too long, maybe if you got a place and just came during the day..."

His words stunned her. She gasped and stepped back. "If you want out yourself tell me now. Just say it, Alex. I'll understand."

"I don't want that." His voice was suddenly stern. "We'll proceed as we agreed. The summer. Until school begins." He cocked his head. "Do you agree?"

Maggie swallowed miserably. "I do." The hollow words hung in the air.

They went downstairs together, miles apart emotionally. Outside, Ruth was directing waiters and waitresses, and Kate was kneeling on the patio with the next door neighbor's cat.

"Excuse me, Mr. Harrison? Ms. Weller?"

The two of them turned to a young man draped in a black robe that hung to about the middle of his shin. His legs were bare and on his feet he had a pair of brightly colored high-top tennis shoes.

Alex turned wide eyes to him. "You are...?" he asked, in dread.

"Reverend Callam Gash." He held out a hand, richly adorned with rings. "We spoke on the phone."

Alex felt Maggie's gaze burning upon his cheek. "Yes." He cleared his throat. "Yes, we did."

Callam Gash extended his hand to Maggie, who looked as if she'd just encountered Jerry Lewis in a tutu. "Callam Gash, Ms. Weller. I'm so pleased to meet you on this wonderful occasion."

She smiled. "Pleased to meet you," she responded

automatically. Her smile became fixed. Alex noticed her tugging gently to release her hand, to no avail. "Are you going to be performing the ceremony?"

"Yes, indeedy." He smiled broadly. "It was a lucky thing I was free." He continued to shake her hand.

Maggie looked at their hands. "Oh, my, what an interesting ring!"

Callam followed her gaze and released her hand. "Oh, I know what you're thinking," he said, touching the large lion's head. "It's an opium ring." He flipped the metal mouth open. "Empty. I don't use it, of course."

"No, of course not." Maggie turned her gaze to Alex. "May I have a word with you?"

Between Callam Gash and Maggie at this moment, Alex wasn't sure who he'd rather remain with. Duty prevailed. "Can you excuse us?" he asked.

"Oh, yes indeedy, yes indeedy." Callam took a champagne cocktail off a passing waiter's tray. "I'll just introduce myself around." His eyes fixed on Ruth and he left them.

"*Where* did Julia find *him?*" Maggie rasped.

"Actually...Julia didn't find him. I did."

"*You?*" She looked at him incredulously. "Are you serious? Where?"

"The Church of the Higher Third, I think it was called. In Silver Spring."

"Church of the..." She looked back at the minister. "Why him?"

"Because the only person who can marry you outside the courthouse is a man of God." He looked at Callam. "Any God."

"What, you couldn't find a nice Presbyterian minister? A Methodist? A Rabbi?"

"I spoke with everyone. Callam Gash was the only one who was free on short notice and who didn't insist on premarital counseling to determine if we were truly in this for the right reason."

"Ah." She nodded slowly. "That was a test we couldn't possibly have passed."

"I certainly didn't want to try. We didn't have time to work our way through the *A* to *Z* of denominations."

She quirked a smile. "He's certainly adding color to things, isn't he?"

Alex let out a heavy breath. "Color," he scoffed. "I didn't want this to be *bland,* that's for sure."

"Alex, *darling,*" a throaty voice cooed behind him. Alex froze. He recognized the voice without turning around. "Hello, Marlene."

He turned to see her dressed in a dark gray dress that buttoned to the collar like a German soldier's uniform.

She reached gnarled hands out to Maggie. "And Margaret. How *good* to see you. I trust Alex has given you the day off?" She laughed.

"A whole week, actually." Maggie smiled, in complete control. "We're so glad you could make it today. This will mean the world to Kate."

Marlene nodded, then fished a cigarette out of her bag. "I wouldn't have missed this for anything."

"Thank you. We're both flattered, aren't we, Alex?"

"Flattered," he repeated.

"I understand you have an interview with the government coming up," Marlene said to Maggie.

Maggie looked at her with what she hoped was a nonchalant expression. "If you mean my citizenship test, that's not for a while yet."

"But it's kind of you to be concerned," Alex said bitterly.

They stood face-to-face like a trio of well-dressed boxers. It was Maggie who finally broke the silence.

"Honey, I think we'd better go and greet the rest of the guests." She slipped an arm around his waist.

The touch surprised him.

"Many people are starting to arrive," Maggie said with a little more force. She tightened her arm.

"Excuse us," Alex said to Marlene.

Marlene took a long drag on her cigarette. "Certainly. If you could just show me where Father Kingsley is."

"Father Kingsley isn't here."

"Not here! Why, who is performing the ceremony?"

"The, ah, Reverend Gash," Alex said. "You'll know him when you see him, I'm sure." He gave a curt nod. "We'll be seeing you."

As they walked away, Maggie's arm slipped back to her side and stayed there.

As more people arrived, the party became a blur to Maggie. Faces zeroed in on hers like fighter pilots, introduced themselves or were introduced by Alex, then swooped away as quickly as they came, flying off undoubtedly to draw and discuss their conclusions about her.

It was hardly the wedding she had dreamed about as a girl in England.

But things were never quite the way one thought they would be. Take Alex. He was very much like her dream-groom, except for the tiny detail about them not loving each other.

She thought about her parents and wondered if her father had been her mother's dream come true once upon a time. It was difficult to imagine, since her mother had spent so much time pining over his absence. Like Alex, Miles Weller had spent an inordinate amount of time working, despite the fact that in the end it meant nothing. His wife had come second to that and his daughter…well, Maggie had been very low in that hierarchy. She sometimes wondered if he'd cared about her at all.

So here she was repeating the heartbreaking cycle of caring for a man who didn't—and perhaps *couldn't*— care for her back. And just as a father was supposed to love his daughter, a husband was supposed to love his wife. She had to be insane, letting herself in for that all over again.

But this time there was a difference. This time there was Kate. And if Maggie couldn't stop her own cycle of unrequited love, she might at least be able to help break Kate's.

Noon came and everyone congregated around the trellis they had set up as a garden altar. When Callam took his place in front of it, Maggie could have sworn she heard a collective gasp from the crowd behind her. She closed her eyes for a long moment, praying to make it through the ceremony without passing out.

Callam's voice had an unexpected boom when he needed it to. "Friends," he announced, "we are gathered here to join Margaret and Max in wedded bliss."

A murmur waved over the crowd.

"Alex," Alex muttered to the man. "My name is *Alex*."

Callam watched the crowd's reaction with apparent satisfaction. A benevolent smile pasted itself across his face. "Margaret and Max have asked that you be here to share the joy and happiness just as they hope you will be there—''

''Excuse me,'' Alex said, louder this time. ''I think you mean *Alex*. Margaret and *Alex*.''

Callam looked at him this time and nodded, displaying no sign whatsoever of embarrassment. ''Just as Margaret and Alex hope you will be there in times of need. For that is the definition of friendship and love.''

Maggie took a shuddering breath and closed her eyes again. Immediately she felt Alex's hand on her arm, steadying her. For a second she stayed still, tingling under his touch. She opened her eyes and looked at him. He was already looking at her. When their eyes met his mouth twitched into a smile so brief she wasn't sure it had happened.

She sighed inwardly. His blue gaze was intense, but it was that tiny smile that did it—his magnetism was overwhelming. She straightened her back and scooted ever so slightly toward him, allowing herself that one small concession.

''Alex,'' Callam said, with a serious look. ''Do you accept Margaret as friend, mother, sister and lover?''

Stunned, Maggie glanced at Alex and saw in his wide-eyed expression, a mirror of her own shock. A moment later, he stammered, ''I do.'' Then looked to her as if to say *I didn't know it would be like this.*

''Margaret,'' Callam said, turning the same serious look to her. ''Do you accept Alex as friend, father, brother and lover?''

She sensed, rather than saw, Alex's bulk as he shifted his weight and tightened his hold on her arm. The wind carried the familiar scent of his cologne to her and for some reason that one detail weakened her. As ludicrous as the vows sounded, they were intended as gravely as any others would have been. In answering, she was promising an awful lot.

They both were.

"I...I do." She felt her face grow warm.

"May I have the rings?"

Rings! Maggie felt cold rush over her. She glanced at Ruth, who shrugged and showed her bare hands. Maggie hadn't thought Alex would wear a ring. Apart from that, she hadn't given the matter of rings—specifically one for her—any thought at all.

Alex had, evidently. He reached into his vest pocket and held a gold ring out to Callam. The minister then turned to Maggie and asked, through his teeth, "Where is Max's ring?"

She shrugged helplessly, hoping the crowd couldn't tell exactly what was going on.

"We didn't get one for me," Alex said. "Go ahead with that one."

"But I must have two rings," Callam objected. "The success of the ceremony depends on it." He gave a slight snort of disgust then said, "Never mind, you can borrow one of mine." He wrenched the opium ring off his finger and held it high in the air with the gold ring for Maggie.

"Lord around us, please smile upon these rings, symbols of everlasting togetherness for these two people."

With one of them an opium ring, it didn't bode well for the future, Maggie thought.

Callam went on to cry something that sounded like, "Wa, wa, wa." Then he handed the rings to Maggie and Alex.

"This exchange of rings means that you will live together always in truth." He nodded to Alex.

Gently Alex took Maggie's fingertips. Her nerves tingled with the contact. Time seemed to stand still. He slid the ring on, that small touch sending shivers down Maggie's spine. Her breath caught in her breast. When the ring was on, he paused, still holding it. Half wondering if he was going to take it off again, she looked at his face, his dark eyelashes lowered as he looked at her hand. Then he let go and looked to the minister.

Maggie followed his gaze to Callam, who nodded at her. Still barely breathing, she took Alex's strong hand in hers. For just a second, his fingers curled around hers and he squeezed lightly. She looked into his eyes. He looked calm, and she instantly felt more relaxed. She took the hideous silver ring and tried to slip it onto Alex's ring finger. It stopped at the knuckle. She struggled with it for a moment, then gave up, leaving it where it stopped.

She grimaced at Alex, who nodded almost imperceptibly.

Callam took a deep, satisfied breath through his nose and smiled at the two of them. "May the winds of heaven blow happiness your way always." He raised his eyes to the crowd. *"Jojinki hoopska ra."*

Silence.

Looking a little concerned, Callam opened his arms. "With me, ladies and gentlemen, *jojinki hoopska ra.*"

There was an awkward muttering of sounds from the crowd.

Apparently mollified, Callam said, "May the winds of heaven always blow good luck your way. You are man and wife." He then let out what sounded like a cross between an ancient tribal shriek and yodeling. When it ended he looked at Maggie and Alex expectantly. "Aren't you going to kiss?"

They turned to each other. Alex's mouth curved into

a smile that she wasn't sure was real. The moments stretched interminably as he bent toward her and placed his lips on hers.

The kiss held nothing. It wasn't as before, in the hallway, or at the racetrack, or on the terrace just the night before. There was no emotion, no passion.

He was doing exactly as she asked, she realized. He was keeping their relationship impersonal.

The kiss only lasted a moment, but Alex didn't release her right away. An extra heartbeat passed before he let her go.

A loud round of applause rippled, started by Ruth. As Maggie and Alex walked down the center aisle, she thought she detected some residual surprise on a lot of faces, but Ruth was alight.

"Excellent," she said in a stage whisper as they passed. She gave Maggie the thumbs up. "It was perfect."

Considering how the rest of the day had gone, Maggie should have anticipated the cats.

It began with one. Kate had been playing with it before the ceremony, so when it jumped onto the buffet table and went for the chicken wings, Maggie shooshed it off without a thought that there would be a problem.

But the cat came back. And it brought another cat. Pretty soon, there seemed to be cats everywhere.

"What's going on here?" Alex whispered, catching Maggie by the punch bowl. "Did they make catnip surprise or something?"

"They seem to want the chicken wings," Maggie answered. "I don't know what to do about it."

"I do," Alex said after a minute. "We'll post children by the table. They'll love being in charge of keeping the cats away.'' With that he hurried off to recruit everyone under five feet to stand guard at the table.

It worked fairly well. Until Maggie found herself locked in a conversation with Marlene Shaw next to the hummus plate.

''What exactly are your honeymoon plans, dear? I...I...I—choo!'' A sneeze burst forth from her. She sniffed. ''Excuse me. Do you have pets?''

''No,'' Maggie began.

''Are you planning to go to the house in the Cayman Islands? Sandra always loved the place.''

Maggie looked down just as a small black paw darted out from under the tablecloth at the ground. She forced her attention back to Marlene. ''I think Alex is trying to work something into his schedule, but we're not sure what.''

''Surely you'll at least be going away for the night tonight.'' She narrowed her eyes. ''Wedding night, and all.''

''We've decided not to go away.'' Maggie thought fast. ''For us, home is the most romantic place. Later in the summer we'll take a vacation with Kate.''

''Kate will be joining you on a honeymoon?'' the older woman asked disapprovingly, punctuating her question with two more sneezes.

The paw darted out again, coming within millimeters of Marlene's ankle.

''No, that will be a family trip,'' Maggie said stiffly. ''Perhaps to Disney World or someplace like that.''

''Oh, dear.'' Marlene clucked in mock sympathy while rummaging through her handbag. She produced a handkerchief and pressed it to her reddening nose. ''This doesn't sound like a typical— Aarrgh!''

It happened in a rush. The cat's paw slipped out

again, this time catching Marlene on the ankle. To make matters worse, the tiny claws got stuck in her stocking.

"*Aaah!* Get this beast off of me! A-*choo!*"

The plate she'd been holding hurled into Maggie's chest. Salmon mousse plopped down into her bra.

"Get it away!" Marlene danced around like a wind-up toy, the poor cat clinging to her foot and wailing like a banshee.

"Mrs. Shaw, if you could just hold still for a moment." Maggie bent down and followed foot and cat with her hands. "If you could just be still, I could—"

"For God's sake, get it away!"

Just as Maggie was about to grab the cat, Marlene sidestepped and the chance was lost.

People started walking toward the ruckus.

The cat, with an apparent burst of adrenaline, gave a final scream and dashed into the bushes, taking stocking and skin with him, Maggie was sure.

Marlene stopped moving and stood, one hand on her hat, one fanning herself. "Oh, dear, oh, dear," she repeated, blowing her nose and dabbing at her eyes.

Maggie fought the laughter back. "Mrs. Shaw, I'm so sorry."

By now a crowd had gathered. "Mrs. Shaw, do let me assist you," an older gentleman said, stepping out of the crowd.

Maggie stood up and reached for her arm to lead her to a chair, but Marlene shook it off, turning to the gentleman instead. "I've never experienced such a thing in all my life."

"Neither have I," the man answered soothingly, with a backward glance and a wink to Maggie.

"I must say," Alex's voice said behind Maggie. "You wear your food well."

She turned and he dipped his finger into the salmon mousse on her chest. His fingertip brushed along her skin and Maggie felt the breath catch in her throat. He watched her eyes, then lifted his finger to his mouth. "Delicious."

For a moment she stood in stunned silence, then realized he was playing to his audience. Two could play at that game. She tilted her head and wet her lips. "Care for another bite?"

He ran his fingers slowly across her shoulder. "You should always serve it this way."

"But then I would be at the mercy of your appetite," she said quietly. She wished his flirtation wasn't a show, but she knew it was.

"And I would be at *your* mercy," he responded. "Who do you think would starve first?"

"Maggie, Maggie." There was a tug on the hem of Maggie's dress and she looked down to see a very concerned Kate. "You have food all over you, did you know?"

Maggie looked down then at the mess that had been her wedding dress. It was now a mélange of salmon mousse, hummus, vegetable salad, and butter. She laughed, a little uncomfortably. "So I do. I think perhaps I'd better go in and change." Anything to get away and catch her breath.

"I'll help you," Kate said, with authority.

"No, *I'll* help her." Alex stepped between Maggie and Kate. "You see how your grandmother is doing."

"Okay." Kate ran off, leaving Alex and Maggie alone.

When she looked at him, she saw that the affable humor he'd displayed only a moment before was gone. Instead his expression was dark, and serious.

And most disconcerting.

"Maggie," Ruth called from the terrace. "Grab some more champagne while you're in there."

"Okay." Maggie kept her eyes fastened on Alex. Somehow it seemed vitally important that she figure out what that expression meant.

"After you—" he swept an arm toward the house "—Mrs. Harrison."

Chapter Six

"You look serious," Maggie said, trying to sound cheerful instead of terrified. Had Marlene said something to him? "This is supposed to be a party."

"I have a lot on my mind."

"Are you already having regrets?" she asked, as casually as she could. *Buyer's remorse?* she added silently.

"What's to regret?"

"Marrying a woman you don't love."

"You already know how I feel about that combination. As marriages go, this is a perfect one."

"That's very flattering."

"Don't take it personally."

Well, that was it in a nutshell. It was all nothing personal. "Don't worry, I won't," she assured him.

"Marlene is suggesting we go to the Cayman Islands for three weeks next month," he said, as solemnly as if he were telling her of a death. "She offered to take care of Kate. And of course she suggested it in front of some old family friends.''

''What did you say?''

''I said I had to talk it over with you. If you'd like to go, you can. I'll say business delayed me at the last minute.''

Maggie shook her head. ''This arranged marriage business is hard enough to get used to. I don't think I could stomach a honeymoon alone.''

''Then I'll say you have something else in mind.''

''Why do you have to say anything?''

''Because I don't know who her contact is at the INS, but it doesn't look real good if we're not interested in a honeymoon.''

''I see.'' The lie of their marriage was already getting to her. ''Then say whatever you need to.'' She turned and went upstairs to change.

When she emerged ten minutes later, she ran into Alex again on the stairs.

''Ruth mentioned they were out of champagne,'' she said, trying not to notice how fantastic he looked. ''Should I go to the wine cellar and get some more?''

He shook his head. ''I'll go.''

''No, I can do it.''

''Go back out and enjoy the party.''

Facing all those people again as Mrs. Harrison, accepting the congratulations and gifts, was about the last thing she wanted to do. ''You go back out,'' she insisted. ''Most of them are your friends. They'll miss you more than they'll miss me.''

He took some keys out of his pocket, looked through them, found the one he wanted and said, ''I'm going.'' Then, with a sudden flash of perception he added, ''You can come with me if you want to.''

Obviously he was no more anxious to return to the celebration than she was.

Maggie followed as Alex led her down a creaking stairway to the cellar. He stopped at a small, thick wooden door.

"This part's a little tricky because there's no light in the hall, just in the wine cellar."

Maggie looked in at the dark cavern and felt a twinge at her back. "Not very well designed."

"Not designed for electricity, anyway. It's the oldest part of the house. I keep meaning to fix it but I don't come down here enough to really feel compelled. Just follow me through." He paused, then added, "Maybe you should put your hand on my back and I'll guide you."

With a pounding heart, Maggie reached out and laid her hand on his shoulder. Warmth radiated from under his cotton shirt and she could feel the ripple of muscle beneath. She curled her fingers tightly against him.

He stopped at a small wooden door and she heard the keys jingle in the dark. Then the door creaked open and they took a silent step into the entry.

Alex stopped as soon as they were through. "Be careful not to close the—"

His sentence was interrupted by the heavy click of the wood door.

"—door."

Maggie realized her mistake immediately. She was glad in that endless moment, that he couldn't see her face because of the dark. "Don't tell me we're locked in," she said. Her voice was more shaky than she'd thought it would be. "Please don't tell me we're locked in."

"Well, that rules out the most obvious topic of conversation," Alex said dryly.

There was a dull snick and a low-watt lightbulb, hanging from the center of the ceiling, sprang to life. "What would you like to talk about?" he added.

"The other way out of here?" she asked hopefully, glancing around at the bottle-lined walls and flagstone floor. She looked to him, a dark silhouette in the pathetic light, and fought an urge to reach for him.

"There is," he began.

"Good."

"It's Julia."

"God." Panic rose in Maggie's breast. "She doesn't even know we're down here."

"If they're out of champagne someone will eventually come down for more."

Maggie looked up. The ceiling was high, and solid stone. There wasn't anything remotely resembling a window. "What if everyone thinks we've gone and leaves?" The room temperature was cool but heat rushed over her and she felt her breathing thicken. "No one else has any idea we've come down here." Her eyes scanned the dark space, taking in all the details.

"Your friend does. She told you to get champagne and you said okay. She'll figure it out."

"Even if she does, *you* have the key."

"Julia has copies of keys to every door in this house. So does Mike." Mike was Alex's driver, handyman, longtime employee and friend. "Don't worry. Actually this is kind of funny."

"Hilarious." Maggie didn't know why that was so easy for him to say, because it definitely wasn't easy for her to believe. "There must be another way out of here." Her eyes darted to the door. There was only one knob and it was on the other side. It was a ridiculous design.

Still, it was worth a try. She rushed over to it and flattened her palms on its cool surface. She gave it a powerful shove but the door didn't budge; it didn't even rattle at the hinges. She shoved again. Nothing. "Bloody thing," she said with a final *whack* with both fists.

"Are you finished?" Alex asked.

She turned to him. "For the moment."

He was oddly calm. "I had a party here once and a hired waiter was stuck in here from Saturday night to Monday morning. If there was another way out, I'm sure he would have found it."

"Oh, my God," Maggie groaned, leaning her back against the door. "We're going to die."

"Die?" The word came out with a laugh. It figured he would finally lighten up now, at the end. "Where did you get that?"

She wanted to slap his calm face. "We'll run out of air in no time."

His eyebrow raised a fraction. "That's not likely."

"You don't think so?"

"No, we're much more likely to starve first." He smiled but Maggie didn't think it was all that funny.

"You die of thirst before starvation," she said, correcting him halfheartedly. "We'll die of thirst."

He glanced around at the collection of wine surrounding them. "Have you suddenly become a teetotaler?"

She flashed him a look. "Did you happen to bring a corkscrew with you?" She didn't wait for an answer, but she couldn't help smiling. "Stupid luck, being trapped in a wine cellar with no corkscrew."

"Champagne doesn't need a corkscrew."

This announcement served to partially diffuse Maggie's panic. "And it's not just for special occasions," she said wryly.

He laughed. "There's the spirit. No pun intended."

She leaned against the wall miserably. "How can you be so calm about this?"

"The deed is done. Why worry about it now?" He looked deeply into her eyes. "In fact, this gives us a chance to go through the drill, learn more details about each other for the INS interview."

She swallowed, and held his gaze. "One would almost think you'd locked us down here on purpose."

"If you recall," he said softly, taking a single step toward her, "it was *you* who locked us in here."

Finding no response to that, Maggie again looked around the room. "Whatever." She turned and stared at the door for several seconds.

He took another step toward her and brushed his finger across her cheek. "I promise you that Julia will figure it out before long. She was there the time the waiter got stuck in here. She'll remember that when we don't reappear."

"You seem pretty sure of that."

"I am."

"But you can't be so sure of what another person will do."

He looked at her. "No, but you can hope."

And hope and hope and hope. Looking at him, the entire room seemed to recede into blackness. There was only Alex. She couldn't drag her eyes away from his.

"I guess you're right." Desperately she turned and looked helplessly at the door. "Would it do any good to knock?"

"None at all. How about some champagne?" His

breath was warm on the back of her neck, stimulating and unnerving her at the same time. She wanted suddenly to lean back against him but she turned to face him instead.

"I'd love some."

"I propose we take this opportunity to get to know each other better," he said, walking to a small cool box in the corner that held chilled champagne. "After all, we're married now." He took out a bottle of vintage 1985 Roederer.

"In name only."

"Exactly. So tell me something I need to know about you. Have any allergies?"

Maggie sighed. She never thought she'd spend the hours after her wedding telling her husband her medical history. "I have no allergies. You?"

"None." He ripped the foil off, untwisted the wire hood and opened the bottle in the palm of his hand. There was a hearty pop, and a fine mist of effervescence snaked up from the top of the bottle. "Now I'd like to propose a toast." He held the bottle up. "To Maggie's wedding." He handed it to her.

"*Maggie's* wedding? What about Alex?"

"Weddings always belong to the bride," he reminded her.

She frowned for a moment then raised the bottle. "Very well. To my wedding." She took a sip, then one more. It was the driest of champagnes, crisp and toasty. "Mmm, this is good." She extended the bottle to him.

"No, thank you," he said. His eyes never left hers.

She frowned. "You don't want to drink to our wedding?"

He gave a single shake of the head. "I'm not thirsty."

"Alex, are *you* a teetotaler?"

"That sounds like a little old lady," he joked.

Maggie didn't laugh. "This is a thing with you, isn't it?"

He leaned back and sighed. "Why do you say that?"

"I noticed you didn't drink to the toast outside, either. You had a glass and you even raised it to your lips, but you didn't drink."

"Would you prefer an alcoholic?" he asked dryly.

"Of course not. I don't care if you drink or not."

"Good."

She persisted. "But are you *ashamed* of not drinking?"

He laughed. "Maybe I don't like champagne."

"You can tell me to mind my own business if you want, but I think there's something going on with you that you're not saying."

"Mind your own business," Alex said with a smile.

"I'm the hired wife, remember? Isn't that the job description?" She smiled right back.

He stretched his arms over his head then ran a hand over his neck muscles. Finally he looked back at Maggie and said, simply, "My father drank—a lot—and there's no one on earth I've ever hated more."

The unexpected confession startled her. "Oh, Alex. I'm so sorry. Here I was being flip about the whole thing and..." Her words trailed off but she laid a hand on his arm.

He put his hand on top of hers. "Don't worry about it. This wound isn't fresh, it's just sort of...chronic."

There was a brief, bleak look in his eyes that pulled at her heart. "Do you want to talk about it?"

"No."

She nodded and looked away. None of her business, of course. "Okay."

He heaved a long breath. "When I was a boy, my father was hardly ever even around. I can see now that it was a blessing that he was gone but at the time it wasn't easy."

"I know," Maggie said sympathetically, hoping he would continue.

"My mother worked twelve hours a day with double shifts as a waitress. He drank most of her take-home pay. When he drank he had a violent temper. My mother and I were his targets."

Maggie remembered the scar on his shoulder and her eyes drifted to the spot.

"You noticed," he said, following her gaze. "That scar was his handiwork."

"My God, Alex, no."

"I once made the unforgivable mistake of breaking a glass in the kitchen. He…showed me the dangers of broken glass. My mother was at work. She didn't know until much later."

Maggie bit down on her lip and shook her head.

"When the money ran out, so did he. My mother made sure there was always food, even if it was only boiled dried beans, but there were a lot of other necessities lacking. Believe it or not, there were whole weeks when I couldn't go to school because I had no shoes to wear." He laughed wryly. "Sounds sort of ludicrous, doesn't it?" He raised his foot. "See this?"

She looked at the smooth leather shoe he indicated. "Yes."

"Four hundred and fifty dollars." He looked at her with a wry smile. "That would have gone a long way with Mom in those days. Now I'm walking around on it like it's nothing.''

''Does that make you feel guilty?''

He looked surprised. ''No. It makes me feel great. Because Kate is, too, by God. She'll never want for anything.''

''Except a father,'' Maggie said gently. ''All that working and providing still deprives her of a relationship with her father.''

''That's why I hired you.''

Maggie felt as though she'd been slapped in the face.

Alex continued. ''I'm providing *everything* she needs, everything I never had. Even the attention. She'll only see me at my best.''

''That sounds noble but stupid. You're missing the point.''

He laughed derisively. ''Maybe. It wouldn't be the first time.''

''You don't need to avoid being with Kate in order to be a good dad. You are not your father,'' Maggie said. ''You're not *like* your father. Not in the way you're thinking, anyway.''

He looked at her steadily, then said in evenly measured syllables, ''You don't know that.''

''Yes, I do.''

He leaned back against the wall and looked straight ahead. Long minutes passed before he spoke again. ''Do you remember when we met?''

Maggie was taken aback by the unexpected question. ''Yes,'' she said. ''Your secretary called the Montessori Institute to find out if any of the students might be interested in this job.''

''I talked with eleven other women from that school. No one else even came close.''

Maggie's mouth suddenly felt dry. "I'm glad you thought I was trustworthy."

He was silent for a moment. "I thought you were pretty."

Maggie's face burned like a schoolgirl's. "You did?"

"I still do."

"Thanks." That sounded so inadequate. "Though that's not a very good criterion for a nanny."

"That had nothing to do with why I hired you."

"Why *did* you pick me?"

He drew in a slow breath. "I don't know. You seemed to fit somehow. Everyone else I interviewed seemed to feel uncomfortable. It was like having guests. You...you seemed to be at home here."

"Yes...for some reason it felt that way to me, too."

Another long silence passed. "You don't think much of me as a father, do you?"

"I think of you more as an employer." She tried to smile.

"Do you think you could ever think of me as a husband?" His quiet voice went rough on the word *husband.* It was impossible to tell whether it was because of emotions or allergies from all the dust in the cellar.

Maggie's heart pounded an unsteady rhythm in her chest. "I'll give the job my best shot."

Their eyes met and he moved toward her without dropping his gaze. Attraction buzzed between them and this time Maggie didn't fight it.

Wordlessly he reached out and ran his hand to the back of her head, smoothing her hair. The trail of his touch burned a line of tingling nerves. Slowly, deliberately, he lowered his lips onto hers. The kiss was tentative at first, but Maggie responded hungrily. The champagne had diminished her common sense. Her willpower was fading. It was okay to indulge for a moment, to pretend this was real. For a moment.

She slipped her arms around his back and ran her hands along the powerful muscles. He moved closer and their teeth knocked. Both of them smiled against each other, but only for a moment.

Maggie shifted and he tightened his hold on her. She parted her lips in invitation and he deepened the kiss, plunging his tongue into her mouth, finding hers. She met it, drinking in the taste of him. The light spicy scent of his cologne tickled her nose.

He ran his tongue along her lips, then kissed her cheek, her chin, and a path down her neck.

She moved her hands to his chest and slipped them underneath his shirt, accidentally popping several buttons. When they ticked to the floor, she pulled back a moment in surprise. "I didn't mean to—"

"Forget it," he murmured against her throat. His voice vibrated against her skin, sending chills down her spine. Then he kissed his way to the hollow of her throat.

Maggie ran her hand across the ancient scar on his shoulder and leaned her head back, reveling in the exquisite pleasure of his lips burning a path along her skin. A flick of his tongue against her throat sent her whole body into shivers of excitement.

Flashes of light burst behind her closed eyelids. She wanted more. But she shouldn't. As intoxicating as this was, she had to draw the line. Soon.

"You taste like wine. I may have to reconsider my abstinence," Alex whispered.

Her throat was dry. "We...shouldn't..." she managed to say, between breaths.

He moved his lips back to hers, and she felt like an

ice cube melting into the floor at high speed, with heat and cold rushing over her simultaneously.

Deftly he slipped his hands underneath her shirt and ran his palms along her ribs. Every single inch of Maggie tingled. Gathering all her will, she drew back.

At that moment there was a noise in the hall outside the door.

"Alex? Are you in there?" It was Julia.

Alex and Maggie locked gazes. He looked amused and chagrined. It was a stark contrast to the panic and embarrassment she felt.

Maggie hurried to straighten her clothes. Alex gave her a quick, devilish smile before calling, "We're here, Julia. Do you have the key with you?"

"Yes, I have it somewhere here. Give me a minute, let me look."

"Thank God she's here," Maggie said, straightening her dress.

"Yeah, I've been pretty miserable," Alex said, standing up.

Maggie looked at him while patting her hair into place. *"That,"* she said, "was a mistake. Thank goodness Julia came along."

The key scraped in the lock. "This is bad timing," Alex said.

"This is divine intervention." Maggie corrected him.

The door flew open and Julia said with a smile, "If you didn't want to socialize, you shouldn't have had a party."

"Did we miss the whole thing?" Alex asked with a smile.

"I'm afraid so. People assumed the two of you had stolen off to some private hideaway, though I don't think this was what they had in mind."

"How did you know to come look for us?" Maggie asked.

Julia turned to her. "Ruth mentioned something about you getting champagne. We put two and two together." She turned back to Alex. "Remember that waiter last year?"

He nodded. "I was telling Maggie about it."

Julia dropped her key into a pocket. "Well, pretty much everyone has gone, and the help is upstairs cleaning up. The drawing room is filled with gifts."

"Where's Kate?" Maggie asked.

"Ruth took her upstairs to her room. She had quite a lot of cake and sweet soda and now she has a tummy ache."

Maggie frowned. "I'd better go check on her. Thanks for the rescue, Julia."

"You're welcome," Julia said. Turning back to Alex she said, "You said you had some important dictation you wanted to do this afternoon, are you sure you want to do that?"

Maggie walked away, unwilling to hear his answer, feeling her stomach twist into a sick knot. He had actually arranged to have his secretary stay for a couple of hours after the wedding so he could do work?

It wasn't surprising.

What was, was the fact that she had set herself up for such disaster by giving in to him. Married or not, his interest was all about the physical and hers kept getting mixed up with the emotional.

She had to take control, here and now. She was an employee. Feelings didn't matter with Alex. He had made that clear several times. And if she slept with him, knowing that, she would be nothing more than his hired companion...a euphemism for prostitute.

Maggie Weller had more pride than that, that was for sure. From now on, it was going to be strictly business. She wouldn't let her feelings get in the way again.

She took broad steps across the hall. Her resolution was firm. Alex Harrison must never know she wanted him.

When Alex went to the kitchen fifteen minutes later, he found Maggie there, filling a plate with plain toast and graham crackers.

"For Kate?" he asked, with a nod toward the plate.

"Yes. She's feeling somewhat queasy." She closed the graham cracker box and looked at him. "We have to talk."

His stomach tightened. "About what, exactly?"

"That was a good talk we had today, Alex, a really good talk. It helped me to understand a little better why it's so difficult for you to get close to her. I don't know exactly what the solution is, but I'm more convinced than ever that it's possible for you to be an active parent." She poured the ginger ale into a glass.

"You make me sound like a new toy. An *active parent* doll."

"Do you have any idea how important this is?"

"You've given some indication. Go on."

She returned the soda to the refrigerator and put the cracker box back in the pantry. "Well, after what happened between us today... I don't think you have the emotional energy right now to invest in two relationships. Kate obviously should take priority."

Embarrassment warmed his face. "I didn't know you and I had a relationship that would require *emotional* energy," Alex said as coldly as he could.

Maggie flushed, too. "I didn't mean... Of course not. We don't."

"Good. Then we understand each other." He shoved his hands into his pockets and walked across the floor.

Maggie put the plate and glass on a tray. "As I was going to say, Kate needs to spend more time with you. Much more. Now, she was resting when I left her." She held the tray out to him. "Why don't you take this to her?"

"That's *your* job."

"Yours, too."

"You can take it up to her. I'll come see her later, when she's finished."

Maggie's keen eyes stayed on him. "I think you should take it up. I think it would mean a great deal to her."

He shifted. "She's comfortable with you and she's not with me." Ever since the incident with the baby bird, he'd been very careful not to put himself in another position where Kate might react negatively to him. He hoped that if she got out of the habit of reacting to him with fear, she might actually start to warm up to him.

"She will be comfortable with you."

"Now isn't the time to push it."

"Okay. You're the boss. If you're too nervous to take it to her—"

Alex frowned. "Who said I was nervous?" Was Kate picking up on that, too? Was she afraid of him because she knew he was a little...well, afraid of her?

Maggie looked at him, wide-eyed. "Aren't you? Isn't that what this is about?"

"No."

She nodded. "Oh, I see." She let the words hang there.

"Fine. I'll do it." He took the tray from her. "Will you be coming up?"

"I'll be up eventually." She smiled warmly. "Don't worry, she'll be glad to see you."

Chapter Seven

It was all Maggie could do to stay in the kitchen instead of following Alex up to Kate's room. She was amazed that he'd let her goad him into going, and she was eager to see how the interaction went. Yet at the same time she was uneasy. She'd sent Alex specifically to replace her in tending the ill child, but she knew how uncomfortable he was about doing it.

But he had to start sometime, didn't he? The sooner the better.

She hoped with all her heart that Kate would start to see her father as someone she could count on and turn to with all her problems and needs. He would get so much out of that, too.

The irony of it was, once they got their relationship worked out, Maggie would no longer be necessary. She was working for her own obsolescence.

Maggie sighed and walked slowly out of the kitchen into the hallway. As much as Kate needed Maggie, Maggie needed Kate. She had grown to depend on that cheerful smile to greet her in the morning; she loved that tiny voice raised in make-believe play. Her heart would break on the day she looked at the splashed paintings and glue projects on the refrigerator for the last time.

There was also Alex now. She'd nearly fallen for him—despite a lifetime of knowing better. Julia had come to the wine cellar in the nick of time. From now on, Maggie was going to keep her wits about her.

Definitely.

She stopped at the entrance to the drawing room. Julia hadn't exaggerated: every surface and an entire corner of the floor was covered with prettily wrapped wedding presents. There was a bouquet on the table by the door. A bright card in the flowers said Good Tidings For A Happy Lifetime Together. Maggie leaned against the doorway and closed her eyes. A knot rose in her throat and sat there. She took a deep breath, and then another, but nothing stilled the trembling of her heart.

A happy lifetime together.

Those kisses—in the hallway, on the terrace, in the wine cellar—were warning signals that she had foolishly ignored. Her troubles were not with what Alex wanted; they were with what she wanted. Even now her heart pounded with remembered passion as she thought of Alex in the wine cellar, of his tongue running along her skin, and what could have happened if Julia hadn't come along to let them out.

They would have made a huge mistake, that's what. Maggie might as well have drawn a bull's-eye across her heart. She ran her hand across the back of her neck, where memory had tingled a moment before. It was just physical, she tried to tell herself. If she and Alex had gotten together it would have been a brief remedy for purely physical desire. But some small part of her whispered, *It probably would have been wonderful.*

But it would have been a mistake.

It wasn't part of their agreement.

It wasn't going to happen again.

And she wasn't going to think about it anymore.

"Maggie!" Kate's shriek from above startled her out of her thoughts. "Maggie!" It rang again.

She shook the fog out of her mind. "Kate?" she called, running through the hall to the stairs.

"Maggie!" the child cried again.

When she got to the door of the bedroom, she saw Alex standing by the bed clutching the tray and looking panicked. "It's all right," he said, looking around. He set the tray on the bedside table and sat uneasily on the edge of the bed. "Daddy's here. It's just a nightmare." He reached out to touch Kate, but she rolled away.

"Kate?" he said quietly. "I'm here. It's all right now, I won't leave you."

There was no reaction from the child. She was suddenly quiet, and her sides raised and fell in rhythm with her breath.

Maggie realized that Kate was asleep. She'd probably been asleep the whole time. She'd been crying out in some dream. Crying out for Maggie.

Alex must have sensed her presence because he got up and stepped into the hall, shutting the door halfway. "It seems she wants you," he said with a slight tremor in his voice. "She had her eyes open but she didn't seem to recognize me."

Maggie's heart filled with sadness for him, not for the truth of the matter, but for what she knew he was feeling. "The doctor calls those dreams 'night terrors.' They don't really mean anything but they're pretty scary the first time you see them. Children seem to be awake but they're hysterical and there's absolutely no calming them down.''

''I suppose I should know that already.'' His voice was tight. ''I had no idea what was going on.''

''You learn as you go. The important thing is that you're here.''

He stiffened. ''The important thing is that *you're* here. She needs *you*.''

Maggie shook her head helplessly. ''It was a dream.''

''She was calling your name.''

''It doesn't mean anything.''

He stood up. ''How long are you going to keep saying that?'' he asked. ''Why won't you acknowledge the fact that this child sees you as a mother, needs you like a mother. Hell, she sees you as mother *and* father. You've heard her say she hates me. Who could blame her? Bad parenting is a Harrison family tradition.''

Maggie's eyes filled with tears. ''You know she doesn't hate you, no matter how it seems right now. She loves you.'' Her voice was hushed. She didn't want to wake Kate. ''And you're not a bad parent.''

''I am. But don't look so guilty about it. It's my fault and I know it.'' He went to the door and stopped halfway through, turning to look at her. The air around him seemed to tremble. ''I know it,'' he said again.

Maggie went downstairs to Alex's office. His door was slightly open, but she knocked softly anyway.

''May I come in for a moment?'' she asked, peeking in.

Alex was staring out the window. ''Are you going to tell me how to be a father?''

''No.''

He turned and gestured her in. "I can't believe that, but come on in. Have a seat."

She sat. "I want to tell you something about how *not* to be a father. I want to tell you about *my* father."

He sat down on the edge of the desk before her and focused a penetrating gaze on her. "Please, go on."

"Stop me if I tell you something your investigator has already told you," Maggie said with a smile.

"I've told you pretty much all he knew."

"Okay." She took a breath. "When I was really young, around Kate's age, my father had one of the most successful investment firms in all of the U.K. We lived in a pretty generous house in North London, not quite as big as this one but close. Like Kate, I had so many nannies that eventually I stopped trying to remember their names. Like my parents, I just referred to them as 'nanny.'"

Alex didn't speak, but the small softening of his gaze was unmistakable.

Maggie ran a trembling hand through her hair. "My mother tried, but she was so busy being the dutiful wife that she couldn't take much time for me."

"And your father?"

Maggie let out a sigh. "Father was much too busy for a child. He had no interest in it. Except when he wanted to present the family-man image at a party. The rest of the time it was like he didn't exist in my life and I didn't exist in his. When I turned six he sent me off to a boarding school in the north. I saw my parents for a week at Christmas and a month over the summer. That was it."

"This explains a few things. Like why you feel so strongly about Kate's involvement with me."

Maggie took a long, slow breath. "I've spent a lifetime trying to reconcile my feelings about my father. You can never know the pain unless you've been there. To wonder your whole life about something, which everyone else takes for granted, something as simple as a parent's love.''

"Kate knows I love her.''

"Maybe she does. But she has to *feel* like you do.''

Alex stood and walked back to the window. ''Why did you take this job with me? Your family obviously has a lot of money.''

"Had,'' she said. ''Had money.''

He glanced at her. ''May I ask what happened?''

"When I was about eight, my father's business partner ran the business into the ground and left with the cash. We had nothing. We had to give up the cars, the house, everything and move to a small row house in the north.''

"Did your father build the business again?''

"He tried. Lord knows he tried. We saw very little of him for the next couple of years, but all his efforts failed. The simple life wasn't acceptable to him, so he kept trying, harder all the time. Worked himself into an early grave, literally. He died when I was ten.''

"I'm sorry.''

She shrugged. ''It sounds callous but I hardly knew the man. It was like a distant uncle passing away, except for the effect it had on my mother. She was devastated.'' Maggie thought of the money she sent to help support her mother every week. ''Her life never really got back on track.''

"That's a sad story.''

"I don't want my life to be a sad story,'' Maggie said. ''I don't want Kate's to, either. Or yours.''

He turned back to her. "Don't worry about me. I can take care of myself."

"Everyone needs people," Maggie said. "At least some of the time."

"If you need people you get hurt. Ninety percent of the time if you rely on someone they'll let you down."

"So you draw up contracts, to keep them in line."

He splayed his arms. "A man's got to protect himself."

"But at what cost?"

He didn't hesitate one second before answering, "At any cost."

Day two in the life of Mrs. Alex Harrison began awkwardly.

Maggie was awakened from a sound sleep at 7:00 a.m. by Kate, who stood by the bed, tugging on the covers.

"Maggie, why are you in *this* room?"

Maggie rubbed her sleepy eyes. "What? What's wrong?"

"Aren't you and my father sharing a room now?" Maggie was awake instantly. "Married people have one bedroom," Kate went on.

"Kate, that's not necessarily true—"

"And what are all those presents downstairs?"

Maggie didn't question the sudden change of topic. "Wedding presents."

"Can I open some?"

"Sure."

"Are any of them for me?"

"Well, they're for all of us."

"Do you think there are any Power Rangers toys?"

Maggie smiled. "I don't think so. It's mostly glasses and silver things, stuff like that."

Kate screwed up her face. "That's boring. Why would people think I want glasses and silver things?"

An idea hit Maggie. She'd been wanting a way to get Alex and Kate on a new level of understanding and now an answer presented itself. "Actually there might be something really special on the way for you."

"Oh, boy, what is it?"

"It's a surprise."

"When will it be here?"

"Soon," Maggie assured her. "What time are you going to your friend's house today?"

"Mrs. Bond is coming to get me at ten. How long is that?"

Maggie glanced at her watch. "Three hours. That's perfect."

At 2:00, Maggie entered Alex's home office unannounced.

"What a surprise," she said, "to find you working on a Sunday. Oh, sorry."

He looked up, startled, from a telephone call.

An Australian-accented voice droned in his ear. "...if you are going to go ahead with this merger, you have to understand that we take it very seriously. It's going to require a great deal of commitment and hard work to see it through."

Maggie mouthed the words, *I have to talk to you.*

He tried to wave her away but she didn't budge.

"Mr. Harrison?" the tinny voice asked over the telephone wire.

"I'm on an important call!" he whispered gruffly at Maggie.

The small voice on the telephone answered him. "I'm aware of that, Mr. Harrison, I want to know if you're willing to commit to this."

Maggie stood before him, smiling like a coquette. "I'll wait," she whispered.

"Wait outside," he whispered back. "Ah, fine," he said into the telephone. "I'll do whatever's necessary."

"Mr. Harrison, doing what's necessary is not enough. Anyone can agree to that. We need to know that you're willing to go all the way with this," the voice said impatiently.

Maggie walked to the wall opposite him and examined a painting. Suddenly the only figure Alex could concentrate on was hers. She was wearing a blue dress of some sort that hugged her narrow waist and slender hips without squeezing and looking too tight. Her long legs moved gracefully as she sidestepped to look at another painting, next to the first. He thought about how close he'd come to caressing those legs, to feeling them entangled with his own, to feeling that body without the constraints of clothing and propriety.

Damn it.

For a moment, he considered tossing something at her to get her attention so she would leave and let him concentrate on the call. But when her earring dropped to the floor and she bent down to pick it up, he decided that it was best to postpone the call instead.

"I'm willing to go all the way," he said into the phone, then shifted in his seat.

"You're clear on the seriousness of this venture? We don't want to be taken lightly. We're talking about being together for a long time, despite the difficulties we'll undoubtedly face at first. Do you definitely want to take this on?"

Alex stared at Maggie. "I do."

The words seemed to rebound around the room and off the walls.

"Excellent. Let's talk about the terms."

"Jack," Alex said into the phone. "Something's just come up. I'll have to call you back for the details." He hung up the receiver and Maggie turned to him.

"You didn't have to hang up on my account."

"Yes, I did. Now *what* do you want?"

"I had a great idea."

"A great idea? That's what you interrupted me for? I was on the phone with *Australia,* for crying out loud."

She nodded and plopped into the sofa against the wall. "This is really important. It's about Kate."

"Okay." He leaned back and folded his arms in front of his chest. "What is it?"

"I thought we should give *her* a wedding present."

"That's it?"

Maggie nodded.

"Okay, I'll have Julia pick something up. Now, if you'll excuse me, I have to call that guy back."

"No," Maggie said firmly. "This has to be something more special. Something that you put yourself into." She smiled to herself. "So to speak."

Alex sighed. "I suppose you have something in mind?"

"As a matter of fact I do. In fact, I've already picked it up."

"Good." That was simple.

"All you have to do is put it together."

He should have known better than to think it would be that simple. Where Maggie was concerned, things were *never* simple. "What exactly do you mean 'put it together'?"

"It's a playhouse kit." She nodded. "It's the perfect thing."

"A playhouse kit," he repeated.

"Yes, it's a big thing. Really heavy...they had to carry it to the car for me at the store. I couldn't possibly do it myself."

"Is this thing going to need special zoning and an electrician?"

"No, it's just a little wood thing. But it will be fun to fix it up anyway. We've got the whole day."

"We?"

"You and me."

"I can't possibly do this."

"Why not?"

He gestured at his desk and the phone. "Work. I have things to do."

"Please!" She waved her hand. "You can worry about that later."

"It's my *life*."

"*This* is life," Maggie said. "This is much more important than phone calls and computers and paperwork. We're talking about your daughter."

"She's not going to know or care who put the damn thing together. Let me call Mike, he might be willing to do it if I throw a few bucks his way."

"Good Lord, Alex, you think money is the answer to *everything*." Maggie's voice rose with exasperation. "You and I may be living on the same earth but we are *not* in the same world and I don't understand yours at all."

"Is that all?" he asked, like a bored waiter.

"Do you hear anything I say?"

"I hear everything you say. The whole neighborhood

hears everything you say. I just don't happen to agree with it all.''

"You know what? Earlier, when I said you were nothing like your father, I was wrong. You're not abusive and you're not an alcoholic and, yes, you support your daughter, heaven knows. But you're like him in one of the most damaging and despicable ways you can be—you neglect your child. And that,'' she spat, ''is inexcusable.''

Chapter Eight

Alex tried to work after Maggie left, but he couldn't keep his mind on what he was doing. Her words had cut him to the quick.

You're like him.

He *was* like him. Too much like him, at any rate. It was the thing he had tried his whole life to avoid. And now he couldn't turn away from it anymore—he was face-to-face with it. Not because she had said so but because he'd known it. Every time he looked in the mirror he saw not the coppery hair his mother had before she'd gone gray, but the dark, devilish hair of his father. And his hands...that was the worst. Hands he'd known so well, and feared so much, were now his own hands.

Of course Maggie hadn't meant his hair, his face, or his hands when she'd said he was like his father. She'd meant that he neglected his child. She didn't understand that the less Kate saw him, the happier she was. She didn't understand Kate's dismay at being shipped off to live with a father she didn't know. Maggie didn't understand Kate's fear of a large, impending stranger calling himself "father."

Alex understood it. And if Kate didn't want to be around him, he wasn't going to force himself on her. That could only do more damage than good. And he'd done a good job of solving that problem—he'd hired Maggie.

He looked out the window and saw Maggie struggling with the huge pieces of wood that were to compose the playhouse. "Other way," he muttered, watching her try to set up one of the sides. "That's upside down."

She tried to move it and it went crashing to the ground.

He looked at the papers on his desk then back at Maggie. He sighed. He didn't have time to spare. Certainly not the kind of time required to put that damned thing together.

He stood up, briskly rolling up his sleeves. He'd have to help her, at least a little, or there was going to be an accident. He smiled grimly. He had to protect his investment.

When he got to her, she had three nails in her mouth and was leaning against the side panel of wood to keep it upright. "Enjoying yourself?" he asked laconically.

She spit the nails out. "No, as a matter of fact," she answered.

"I thought I hired you as a wife. There was nothing in the contract about carpentry."

She stood back and let the wood fall to the ground again. "Clearly." She wiped a tanned forearm across her brow.

"Need a little help?"

She pretended to look around. "Did you hire someone?"

"Will I do?"

She looked skeptical. "Will you do for what?"

He looked at the pieces of playhouse, then back to Maggie. "Anything. Is there anything I can do that would satisfy you?"

She ran her tongue across her upper lip in an unconsciously seductive gesture. "How hard are you willing to try?"

Their gazes locked.

"I work hard to get what I want," he said, surprising himself.

She met his gaze. "They say you can't always get what you want."

"They also say you get what you need," Alex returned.

She smiled but it was strained. "I think you've got everything you *need* already. You just haven't figured out what to do with it. I told you I'm willing to help you with that."

"You're referring to Kate."

She nodded.

He clicked his tongue, letting the moment of brashly spoken truth pass. He was already regretting his open words. "Okay, I'm here. Let's get this done." He picked up the instructions and after a moment said, "Okay, I've got it. Hand me a flat-head screwdriver, would you?"

She handed him the screwdriver and their hands touched. Neither one let go for a moment, then Maggie pulled her hand back. "You should probably check the instructions. See what you need."

"I know what I need," he said evenly. "The question is, do you know what you need?"

"Are we still talking hardware?" she asked, trying to laugh. "Because I'm just the assistant here."

His gaze was relentless. "I have a couple of hours free this evening. Can we get together and talk about the INS review hearing? We really should have done that before now."

Her breath was shallow. "Okay." She prayed he couldn't hear the pounding of her heart. It was thundering in her own ears.

"Good." He looked back at the sheet of paper. "I need a screw."

Her gaze flew to his.

He pointed at a plastic bag near her feet. "They're there. If you could hand them to me as I need them it would be a great help." There was just the tiniest hint of a smile tugging at the corner of his mouth.

She looked down at the bagful of screws and bolts. "Oh, I see." She pulled the bag open and handed him one.

After that the work went smoothly, although the conversation could have been a lot more comfortable. As the little house took shape, Maggie was amazed at the care he took in putting it all together.

"You're awfully good at this," she said.

"You sound surprised."

"Maybe a little. I've hardly ever seen you outside the office. That is, I didn't know you were so good with your hands." She thought of the wine cellar. Lord, she was putting her foot in it over and over again this afternoon.

He raised his eyebrows. "Glad I could surprise

you." He looked back at his work. "I built a lot of the furniture in that house."

"You're kidding."

The corner of his mouth curled upward. "Surprised again?" He set the screwdriver he was working with down. "If I were another sort of man I would probably be insulted at the shock you display every time I do something that doesn't require a desk. I do have a life outside the office, you know."

"Really?"

He picked up the screwdriver and continued with his work. "A long time ago, I learned that people had expectations of me. They didn't want more, or different. So I've pretty much kept my private self to myself."

She couldn't answer. Two birds whistled their summer tunes in the tree above them.

"Anyway," he went on. "I also discovered, along the way, that work was a real good escape." He met her eyes. "That bothers some wives."

"I should think so."

He nodded and gave a final turn of the screw. "Does it bother you?"

"No."

"Ah." He nodded. "Well—"

"I'm hoping that's going to change," Maggie said. "I'm hoping you'll be spending a lot more time at home, especially with the summer coming up."

"We're not getting into that now." He stepped back from the playhouse. "There."

Maggie watched him looking at his creation. There seemed to be real pride etched in his features.

"She'll like it, won't she?" he asked.

"She's going to love it."

Maggie studied his profile as he assessed the work.

This was a tenderness for Kate that she had never seen before.

He turned to her. "Maggie? Are you all right?"

"Fine." She swallowed. "Why?"

"You look pale. Maybe you should go in." He was at her side in an instant, and slipped his arm through hers. "It's probably the heat. Let me take you in."

She didn't pull away from his touch. "I'm fine."

"Let's get you in anyway." His arm bumped against her shoulder, and he tightened his grip.

Though it was the last thing she wanted to do, Maggie stepped to the side, slipping her arm out from his.

She didn't want to risk her body's reaction to his touch again, no matter what.

Kate hated the playhouse.

Well, maybe she didn't *hate* it, Alex conceded to himself. Looking at her, she actually seemed to be more afraid of it than anything else.

He and Maggie led her out to it the afternoon after they'd built it, full of anticipation. As soon as she saw it, she stopped in her tracks.

"What's *that?*" she cried, her eyes wide.

"It's a house just for you," Alex said.

"Daddy built it," Maggie added.

"Oh." Kate's face fell.

Maggie's brows knit into a small frown. "He worked very hard on it. All afternoon yesterday while you were at Kyra's."

Kate looked from Maggie to Alex. "It's just for me? Only for me?"

He tried to smile reassuringly. "Only for you."

"But I hope you'll let me visit sometimes," Maggie said.

"When?" Her thin voice rose. "A lot?"

"Whenever you invite me."

She looked back at the bright pastel structure. "I don't want it."

Alex met Maggie's gaze over Kate's head but she looked as puzzled as he felt.

"Give it a chance. Don't you want to go in?" he asked, giving Kate a little nudge.

"No!" She looked at Maggie. "Do I have to go in?"

Maggie let out a bemused cough. "No, you don't *have* to go in. Don't you *want* to? I think it's lovely."

Kate rushed to her and wrapped her thin arms around Maggie's legs. "I don't want to go in! I don't want that house! Don't make me!"

Maggie stroked Kate's hair. "Darling, you're trembling. What's wrong?"

"I don't want it!" Kate repeated. "I want to go back in the big house. I want to go to my room."

"All right," Maggie soothed, with an apologetic nod toward Alex. "We'll go in."

Alex watched them go in, then turned back to the playhouse. What was Kate seeing that he and Maggie weren't? It was just a toy.

He frowned. What was it Kate had gotten so upset about that day she and Maggie were playing with the dolls? She thought she was going to be sent away for "being naughty." She'd said it again the day she found the baby bird. She thought if she did anything wrong, her father would want to get rid of her. Even this wonderful toy hadn't taken the edge off her resistance to him. If anything, it had made it worse. She was even afraid of the toy he'd assembled for her.

He looked back at the pink house and the thought came to him.

It was a toy. But did Kate know that? Or did she think of it as proof that he was trying to get rid of her? His chest tightened. Maybe she wasn't afraid of him, as he'd thought for so long. Maybe she just didn't know he loved her!

His own daughter thought he didn't love her. Well, that was one thing he could straighten out himself.

He ran to the house and found Kate and Maggie in the kitchen, having a glass of milk. Kate was still shaky.

"Kate," he said, sitting down at the table across from her. "That house outside, did you know it's just a toy?"

Maggie caught his eye and her own widened.

"A toy?" Kate repeated. "I have to live in a toy?"

There—he'd been right. The horror in her eyes turned his stomach to jelly. "No." He reached out and cupped his hand on her cheek. "No, honey, it's just for you to *play* in. You're not supposed to *live* in it."

"I'm not?"

"No way." He dropped his hand down on top of hers on the table, noticing the cold feel of her small knuckles. "You *live* in this house with Daddy and Maggie. How could you think I'd send you out in the backyard to live?" He knew how she could think that. He'd given her that impression himself, by never telling her how much he cared. "I'd *never* do that."

She didn't look convinced. "But you said it was just for me and you and Maggie would visit sometimes."

"I meant we'd visit in the afternoons if you were playing out there with your dolls and stuffed animals. I want you in this house and in your bed here every night."

Her little shoulders sagged. "So I live *here?*"

He smiled. "Of course. This is your home. That—"

he nodded toward the backyard ''—that's your play-house. For pretending only.''

She looked out the window in the direction of the house. ''It's pretty.''

He looked at her steadily. ''I love you, Katie.'' The surprise in her eyes hurt his heart. ''Just because I don't always remember to say it, doesn't mean it isn't true. I'll *always* love you.''

Kate considered that for a moment, then smiled. A weight was lifted from his chest.

Maggie gave Alex a broad smile, then sat down next to Kate. ''Well, *I'd* like to take a look inside that house this afternoon, how about you?''

Kate nodded tentatively. ''Maybe we could take some dolls out. Just for today,'' she added hastily.

''Absolutely. Why don't you just dash on upstairs and pick a few. We'll take them out to see the place.''

''Okay.'' Kate scraped her chair back and left the room.

''That was brilliant,'' Maggie said when she was gone. ''I never dreamed that was what she was thinking.''

He smiled and shook his head. ''Thank goodness we got it straightened out.''

''*You* got it straightened out,'' Maggie said, pushing her own chair back from the table. ''Good job, Dad.'' She smiled at him sincerely, with real admiration, he thought, and he felt his chest swell like a schoolboy's.

That evening, Alex walked into his bedroom to find piles of Maggie's clothes strewn around the floor. He had a few minutes of wide-eyed bafflement before Kate appeared at his door with another armful of them.

''What are you doing?'' he asked, a little too loudly.

"You and Maggie are married now, so you're going to have one bedroom. I'm helping Maggie bring her stuff in."

His mind raced. Surely Maggie didn't have anything to do with this. "Where is Maggie?"

"At the store. Bess is baby-sitting me. She's downstairs."

"Does Maggie know you're doing this?"

"No." Kate smiled broadly. "It's a surprise."

Alex pinched the bridge of his nose between his thumb and index finger. "Listen, Katie, this is really nice of you, but I don't think you should be going through Maggie's things without asking her first."

"She won't mind. Maggie never minds anything."

"What won't I mind?" Maggie appeared in the doorway holding a drugstore bag. Her gaze immediately fell on the clothes on the floor. "What's going on?"

"I was helping you," Kate said proudly.

"Thank you," Maggie said, her smile fixed. "That saves me a lot of trouble." She turned to Alex and raised her eyebrows.

"Isn't it just about time for Kate to go to bed?"

"Yes." Maggie looked at the clock. "Kate, run and get changed."

"It's early."

It was a half an hour earlier than she usually went to bed, nevertheless Maggie said, "Please get into your nightgown and brush your teeth."

"But—"

"Now, please."

"Okay." Kate skulked off.

When she was gone, Maggie closed the door and whispered, "What are we going to do about this?"

"I think you better stay in here tonight."

"I don't think so."

Alex eyed her. "What are you afraid of?"

"I'm not *afraid* of anything," she lied. Oh, she was afraid all right. She was terrified that her resistance had run out and she would get more involved with him. She was terrified that her feelings for him would grow out of control. She lowered her voice. "But I'm *not* sleeping with you."

"We don't have to sleep."

Maggie straightened indignantly. "Isn't there a saying about the lion and the lamb not laying down together?"

"I thought it was that they may lie down but the lamb won't get much sleep," Alex said blithely. "But that doesn't apply here."

"No. No, it certainly doesn't. And *if* you will recall, we *do* have an agreement."

"Forget the stupid agreement, I'm not planning on taking advantage of you. I'm talking about *sleeping*."

"So am I. I'd like to do that tonight."

"You're not going to change your mind on this particular subject tonight, are you?"

"No."

Alex lowered himself onto the edge of the bed. "Okay, how about this. You make a show of coming in here to go to bed, then when the doors are all closed, you can slip back into your bedroom."

"And in the morning come sneaking back in here before anyone else is up?"

"Yes."

"And I do this for, what, three years?"

"No, you do it until after the INS board has been and gone and we don't run the risk of Kate saying something damaging."

"Can't Kate go to a friend's house that day?"

"They would find that suspicious, don't you think?"

Maggie's shoulders slumped. "This is too much work."

"Look it's just a couple of weeks at the most. We can muddle through."

"Easy for you to say," she muttered.

"It's true. So for now the problem is solved."

The problem returned in the middle of the night. In the form of Kate.

Alex was sleeping heavily when he felt a touch on his arm, and heard Kate say, "Daddy?"

He opened one eye. A crash of thunder opened the other. Lightning flashed and illuminated Kate's worried face. "What is it, Katie?"

"I had a nightmare."

"Oh." He sat up and pulled her into a tight hug. "It's okay now. Sit down and we'll talk for a little while. When you go back to bed the nightmare will be all gone."

"I want to stay in here with you and Maggie." Lightning flashed again and she looked from the bed to Alex. "Where *is* Maggie?"

"Maggie." He closed his eyes and tried to force an answer to come to mind. "Maggie is…getting a glass of water. And an aspirin. She had a headache. You stay right here and I'll go and get her." He turned on the light, propped Kate on the bed and, with a silent prayer, slipped into the dimly lit hall and down to Maggie's door.

He knocked. There was no answer. If he knocked any louder he risked Kate hearing. So he did the only safe thing he could do—he went in.

''Maggie?'' He kept his voice low. He made his way slowly across the room until he got to the bed. ''Maggie?'' he said again. ''Wake up.''

No response.

''Maggie, wake up. We have a problem.'' He bent down to shake her. Unfortunately she was lying on her back and he ended up with his hand on her breast.

That did it.

''Who's there?'' she said, too loudly. Her hand shot out and grabbed Alex's wrist in a viselike grip.

''Maggie, it's Alex.'' His hand was still on her, with her fingers wrapped around his wrist. He didn't move and neither did she.

''Alex?'' The grip loosened.

''Yes.'' Inadvertently he slid his hand down her rib cage. He heard her small, sharp intake of breath.

For a long moment, neither of them spoke. His hand rested on her hipbone and she was as still as a statue. Then she propped herself up in bed and his hand dropped to the mattress.

''What are you doing in here?'' she asked.

''Trying to wake you up.''

''I can tell that. Why? And couldn't you have given me some warning instead of coming right up and mauling me?''

He suppressed a chuckle. ''I didn't maul you.''

''It felt like mauling to me.''

Even in the dark, he knew exactly the haughty look she had on her face. It was one he'd grown very fond of, because she never meant what she was saying when she had that expression on her face. ''Then there's a lot I'd like to teach you about the human touch,'' Alex said, wishing there was time now to explore the subject.

This time her breath shuddered. "I don't think you could teach me anything I don't know."

"Then maybe you could teach me," he mused softly. "Either way that's a classroom I'd like to get into."

She didn't respond. Instead she shifted her weight and asked, in a voice that sounded as if she was trying to steady it, "What are you doing in here in the middle of the night?"

"You've got to come back with me. Kate's in my room."

"Kate? What's wrong?"

"She had a nightmare. She wanted to sleep with us. With you and me. But you're not there."

"Are you making this up?"

That time he knew the facial expression had turned from haughty to cynical. The brows had lowered and the right corner of her mouth had screwed up one or two degrees. He smiled to himself. "I wish I was making it up so I could get you in there under false pretenses, but no, this is the truth. I told her you were getting an aspirin and I'd get you. Come on, we've got to hurry."

The bedsprings creaked. "All right."

When they got back to Alex's bedroom, Kate was sitting on the bed exactly where he'd left her, clutching her teddy bear. She raised wide liquid eyes to them.

"I'm scared," she said in a tiny voice.

Thunder rumbled in the distance.

Maggie sat down on the bed and put her arm around Kate. "What are you scared of? The thunderstorm?"

Kate nodded.

Maggie looked at Alex. "Why do I feel like I should sing 'My Favorite Things'?"

He smiled. "It might help."

"I want to sleep in here tonight," Kate interjected.

Maggie looked at Alex and took a deep breath. "All right." She sighed, and moved to the side of the bed. "Get in." She held the covers open for Kate to get next to her.

She did. Her cold little feet knocked against Maggie's legs as she struggled to get comfortable.

When he saw she was settled, Alex snapped the light off. The bed creaked as he got into it. Maggie had to lean away just to keep from rolling toward him. Fortunately Kate was between them.

Uneasily, Maggie scooted down in the bed, inch by reluctant inch. When she could go no further she laid her head on the pillow. It smelled of his aftershave. She closed her eyes. This was going to be a long night.

Kate snuggled into the crook of Maggie's arm. "Good night Maggie," she said. "G'night, Daddy."

"Good night," Maggie said.

"Good night," Alex repeated, softly.

Maggie stared wide-eyed at the blackness above and started counting sheep.

Sleep didn't come easily to Alex that night and when it did it was restless and nervous.

On the other side of the bed, Maggie tossed and turned. He wondered what she was thinking about.

Kate also thrashed around in bed and more than once Alex felt the soft teddy bear slam firmly into his face. Around three in the morning, Kate sat up.

"What's the matter?" he whispered to her, careful not to wake Maggie.

"I'm hot," she said groggily. "I want to go back to my bed."

"Are you sure?"

She was already climbing out of the bed. "It's too hot here and you two move around too much."

Alex started to get up. "I'll walk you in there."

Kate opened the door. "It's right across the hall," she said, a little patronizingly.

Alex leaned back. "Okay. Good night, Kate."

"'Night, Daddy."

She closed the door and he rolled onto his side. With his eyes adjusted to the dark, he could see the outline of Maggie's form next to him. They were alone. In bed. They were alone in bed together.

This was pretty nice.

He'd certainly thought of it more than once. Ever since that day in the wine cellar, his body had been hungry for more of her. She probably knew it. She certainly seemed worried about it.

So he had to give her the opportunity to leave.

Alex propped himself up on his elbow. "Maggie?" he whispered.

"Mmm?"

He kept his voice very quiet. "Kate's gone back to her room. Do you want to stay here?"

She made some noise in her sleep and rolled over to face the opposite wall.

Sure, he could have tried harder. After all, he knew she was asleep and hadn't heard what he'd said. But, technically speaking, he'd tried.

Very carefully, he draped an arm across her. To his surprise she curled gently into him. What was he supposed to do now? If he moved he would probably wake her up.

That wouldn't be very nice. She obviously needed sleep. So for now, he'd just let her sleep.

* * *

When she first woke up, Maggie couldn't quite figure out where she was. As soon as she did, her eyes flew open and she was fully awake within milliseconds.

How the heck had she ended up here?

She looked around her, at Alex, then anywhere but Alex. She remembered Kate in the middle of the night. But Kate was gone. And Alex, almost naked, was here beside her.

Her body flamed to awareness. After what seemed like hours she found her voice. "Where's Kate?" She pulled the covers tightly around her.

Alex got out of bed and slipped a thin robe on. "She left awhile ago. The housekeeper said the Bonds were here."

"The housekeeper was here, too?"

He laughed. "Think of it this way, it's good for our case." As he moved, Maggie watched the tight V of his torso to narrow hips and possibly the most perfect bum she had ever laid eyes on.

She wanted him. God, she wanted him. And she realized, as one coming out of a long dream, that she had been wanting him for months.

She got out of bed, wrapping a cotton throw around her. "God, who else came through?"

He looked at Maggie with an apologetic smile, apparently unaware of the rushing sensations coursing through her. "No one. And don't worry, you weren't drooling, or talking in your sleep."

But it was all she could do to keep her mind on what he was saying, rather than the expanse of skin and form she'd seen before he'd put on the robe. Thank goodness she didn't talk in her sleep.

She stepped up to him. "If she left an hour ago, how

long have you been up and why didn't you wake me so I could go back to my room?''

He brushed his finger across her cheek. ''It seemed a shame to wake you.''

She closed her eyes when he touched her. Despite her protests to the contrary, she'd been waiting for his touch again. She'd fantasized a million different ways in which it would finally come, but this was outside any of the scenarios she'd made up.

He ran his fingertips down her cheek and across her throat. She took a breath and swallowed.

''You look beautiful, Maggie.''

She tried to smile. ''I *know* that's not true.''

''I want you.''

''We can't.''

''We can.''

''We shouldn't.''

He traced a line from her throat to the valley between her breasts. ''We should.''

''I won't.''

He ran his hand across her belly and, slowly, down. ''I can't force you to do anything you don't want to do.'' He stopped where her thighs were pressed firmly together.

She moved one leg, allowing his touch in. ''Good. Because I'm not going to do this.''

''Okay.''

''I mean it.''

''I hear you.'' His fingers found her sweet spot.

''You're taking unfair advantage of me,'' she murmured halfheartedly. She looked at him under eyelids heavy with desire.

''Fair is fair. You can take advantage of me, too.'' He bent slightly and his fingers worked magic.

Maggie thought her legs would buckle. "I would never..."

"No, never." He traced a line on her arm.

"We can't..."

"But we will."

"We had an agreement," she protested weakly.

His voice became low and throaty. "I think we can negotiate."

She heard, and felt, him move toward her. She opened her eyes and he pulled her into his arms. She didn't resist. This time she couldn't resist. She'd resisted him too many times already and her body simply wouldn't take no for an answer again.

Wordlessly his lips sank down on hers.

This time she didn't hesitate. Her arms, almost of their own accord, pulled him onto her then ran across the hard planes of his back. His breath quickened when her fingers touched his sides. His stomach against hers was as hard as a rock, with washboard ripples of muscle. She ran her fingers over his sides appreciatively, discarding all ideas of stopping the direction of this runaway train.

He pulled back and their lips came apart with a small smack. "We're alone in the house," he said.

"I know."

He pulled the cotton throw off her shoulders and let it fall. "If you want this to stop, you'd better say so now."

She remained silent.

His gaze never wavered as he pulled his robe off and tossed it on the floor.

Her arms were back around him before the material even touched the carpet, and even Maggie was amazed at the urgency of her own desire. His beard scratched against her chin and tickled pleasantly at the nerves beneath. This was Alex. This was the man she'd wanted for what seemed like ages.

Their kisses deepened. Maggie thought she could devour him, heart and soul.

He lowered her gently to the bed.

The soft mattress yielded to their weight and enfolded them in smooth linen. The smell of the laundry soap mingled with Alex's woodsy, manly scent, making Maggie sigh with intoxication. The fabric was cool and smooth against her bare skin.

Chest to chest, his heart pounded a steady, hypnotic rhythm against her breast while his fingers slid down the fabric of her nightshirt and slipped underneath. Cupping a hand on her hipbone, he gently pulled her closer to him. She gasped, then moaned with anticipated pleasure as he lowered his hand to her own core of sensation.

He knew her needs perfectly, as though some instinct guided him and instructed his motions. His fingers, lithe and skilled, moved gently against her, finding the nerve center that shot rivulets of excitement throughout her. He moved them gently at first, then with an increasing tempo.

Physical sensation twirled around the emotions Maggie had kept pent up for so long. Now she let go with abandon. This felt so much like love from him, surely there couldn't be any harm in pretending it was. She had three years to make him love her.

She threw her head back and clenched her teeth to try to bear the exquisite ache, as he trailed his tongue across her cheek and down to her shoulder. Wave after wave of red-hot pleasure pulsed through her until the sensual throbbing joined her heartbeat and exploded in a shower of bliss.

Alex moved over her and kissed her deeply. She encircled his waist with her arms, aware of every twitch of his muscles. He lowered himself down onto her. The light mass of hair on his chest pressed against her breasts, tantalizing, making her arch against him.

"You're so beautiful," he whispered, then lowered his lips onto hers and ran his tongue along the soft skin inside her mouth. She felt the tingling between her legs begin again, with a need so urgent it surprised her.

He kissed her neck, her shoulder, and made a path straight down, circling breasts with his tongue, working his way to the small hard tips. A sensation, such as she had never felt before, gripped her and she realized that she was arching up toward him like a cat.

When he moved back to kiss her mouth, she reached for his hand and tried to guide it to the desperate heat between her legs, but he smiled against her mouth and moved his hand to cup her face, running his thumb back and forth in the hollow under her chin. Desire, need and anxiety intertwined within her, like three strands of a braid.

Alex moved to lay the length of his body across her, his face nestled against her neck. She felt him nudge into her and another wave convulsed her. She ran her hand down his back and pulled him toward her. He entered in one swift movement and a low groan tore from his throat.

Their movements melded together as naturally as if they had been together forever. It was like a perfectly choreographed dance, which they both knew by instinct. To Maggie's surprise, his own craving seemed to grow and increase as he thrust into her over and over until the whole world burst in a blinding white flash.

For a long time afterward, they lay motionless, until their breathing stilled and their frantic pulses faded to regular beats. They lay on their sides, facing each other, and Alex ran his palm along her side. The motion was affectionate, familiar, and Maggie was filled with calm contentedness where, minutes earlier, there had been burning need.

When the phone rang, Alex groaned and said, "Go away."

"You'd better get it, Alex. It could be about Kate."

Reluctantly he rolled over and picked up the receiver. It was his longtime friend and lawyer, Stan Wilkins.

"Alex, there's a problem. I've been concerned about it since yesterday and I don't know how else to handle this except to come right out and say it... It's about the minister who performed the ceremony."

Alex tightened his grip on the receiver. "What about him?"

"Something about him was familiar. I racked my brain and finally remembered this morning. I came into the office to check out my suspicions before calling you..."

"What is it?" Alex prompted.

"It's his license. It expired a year and a half ago. He's been brought in on charges like this before but he doesn't seem to care."

"What are you saying?"

"I'm saying—" he lowered his voice "—Alex, what I'm saying is that *you're not really married.*"

Chapter Nine

"*What?*" Maggie's eyes were wide and her heart pounded a thundering rhythm.

He nodded. "It seems the Reverend Gash isn't licensed. We're not legally married."

"You're not joking, are you?"

He shook his head. "No."

"Could Marlene Shaw have had anything to do with this?"

"I don't think even she is that clever. But if she gets a hold of this information…" He let his words trail off into the conclusion they both drew.

"Great." Maggie leaned back on the bed, but her chest felt constricted. "I'm going to hang for this, aren't I?"

He turned on his side to face her and the bed squeaked under his weight. "No, we'll take care of it. We'll go to the courthouse right away."

"We told the INS we were married. *Married.* And we're *not.*" She held her breath for a brief second, then blew it out. "And we have that interview coming up in three weeks which, by the way, I don't feel all that prepared for. This is the worst thing that could have happened." Inside her heart pounded with grief, rather than fear. She wasn't married to Alex. The small warmth of knowledge that he was her husband had popped and diffused like a balloon.

"Your visa hasn't even expired yet."

Her breath left her. "What?"

"Your visa. It's still valid for a few days. You're not illegal yet."

Yet. A long moment passed in silence. Maggie's eyes burned and she closed them, willing back the tears. He was telling her that she could still leave. And why not? Things were getting better with him and Kate. Maggie had gone a long way in becoming unnecessary. Now Alex saw that, too. She should have known this would happen. Actually, she had known. And she'd given in to her feelings for him anyway.

She had just let herself right out of the frying pan and into the fire. She had known—been *certain*—all along that a physical relationship between the two of them would lead to heartache. She was an employee, nothing more. And now that Marlene had backed off Maggie was less indispensable, Alex had more than one solution to the problem of her expiring visa.

Including the fact that she could go back to her own country.

Maggie pressed her knuckle against her teeth. "So there's still time for me to leave." Her voice was dull, but she didn't want to let him know how shocking and upsetting his suggestion was.

Alex's expression darkened. "You want to leave?"

"Maybe I should. Maybe this is a sign, or a respite

from our making a terrible mistake." She sat up. The covers slipped to her waist and she grabbed them quickly and covered herself.

Alex took a long breath before he spoke. When he did, his tone was hard. "After everything we've been through to make this arrangement, I hope you're not saying you're seriously backing out."

"You mean you don't want me to go?" She may have been happy if it weren't for the iciness of his tone.

"I think we've been through all of this before."

She nodded. Her emotions were reeling from the one second leap from fear that he wanted her to go, to sadness at why he wanted her to stay. She was an employee, hired for a purpose, and probably punishable by law if she defaulted on their contract. She had been a stupid fool to think that he could think any more of her than that. "I guess it would be inconvenient for you if I left here now."

"You bet it would be inconvenient." His sharp tone was a shock.

She felt as if she'd been punched in the stomach. All of her fears had been exactly right. He'd made love with her because she was there and because physically he wanted to, but not because he cared about her or thought anything of her other than what that damned agreement required of her.

How foolish she was to think he would change!

Alex interrupted her thoughts. His voice was hard. "Maggie, we have an agreement. Are you going to hold up your end or not?"

She had to. She had given her word. She'd gone to bed with him of her own free will and she had to live with the consequences. He hadn't broken any promises by not falling in love with her.

"I'll hold up my end of the agreement exactly as we wrote it," she spat, pulling the sheet around her and jerking out of the bed. "And *this* time, I'm going to remember it's business. *Only* business."

"Kate should be here," Maggie said coolly.

Alex leaned back in the hard metal chair and looked around them at the waiting room of the county courthouse. It was Monday morning and the place was mobbed. There were two couples in full formal wedding regalia, and one couple in biker formal wear, complete with nose rings and dog collars. Another couple sat miserable-looking in the corner, wearing jeans and T-shirts. Three of the women he could see were obviously pregnant. He looked at Maggie. "Why?"

She looked around the room. "Well, maybe not *here,* but she should have joined us for the real wedding."

"She has too many other things she's got to try and understand. This—" he nodded toward the biker couple "—may be too much."

Maggie looked around.

"How long is she staying at the Bonds' house?" Alex asked.

"It's a slumber party. They're telling parents to come to pick up around four tomorrow afternoon."

Alex nodded. "Fine, fine."

They were apparently out of small talk.

The desk clerk called a number and Maggie asked, "What's our number?"

He looked at the delicatessen-style paper ticket in his hand. "Nine," he said.

"They just called eight. We're next." She ran her hands up and down her bare arms. Her pale yellow summer dress wasn't warm enough for the icy air conditioning of the government building.

"Are you nervous?" he asked.

What do you care? she wanted to say. "I'm getting used to marrying you," she said instead, turning her face away. She studied the wall beside her. Tears burned in her eyes but the last thing in the world she wanted was for Alex to see them.

"Nine!" the clerk called.

Maggie swiped at her eyes and turned to Alex. "That's us." She stood up.

He stood, and followed her to the clerk. Her footsteps were slow. She felt as if she were walking though mud.

They went into a paneled chapel with several rows of pews and a podium in the front. The clerk, a bored-looking woman wearing what looked like a police uniform, asked, "Do you need a court witness?"

"Yes," Alex answered.

The clerk went to the door and called someone from the back room.

Maggie watched mutely. In just a few minutes it would all be over.

The clerk, joined by another court official, opened a single sheet of paper and read. "Alexander Harrison, do you take this woman to be your lawfully wedded wife, in sickness and in health, for richer, for poorer, as long as you both may live?"

Maggie swallowed and watched Alex with burning eyes.

"I do," he said softly.

The clerk turned to Maggie. "Margaret Weller, do you take this man to be your lawfully wedded husband, in sickness and in health, for richer, for poorer, as long as you both may live?"

A knot formed in her throat. The ticking of the clock on the wall droned loudly. She couldn't find her voice. She couldn't speak.

"Margaret?" The clerk's gaze flicked from her, to Alex, to the witness.

Maggie looked at Alex, who watched her expectantly. She couldn't go through with it. They had a contract, but she knew suddenly that she absolutely could not uphold her end of the bargain.

She couldn't because she loved him. It was completely foolish but she'd gone and fallen in love with him anyway.

It could have been so perfect. They'd had a solid agreement, signed, and notarized. She could have finished her certification and, after Kate started school, she could have gone to work in America. She could have been an American citizen, and had all of the privileges that went along with that.

Now it was all going to be ruined because she had gone and fallen in love.

But there was no way she could agree to a false marriage with him now. There was no way she could live with him, see him every day, and not die of a broken heart.

Alex looked at her and spoke quietly through his teeth. "Maggie…"

At last the words tumbled out of her. "I…I can't do this."

Alex closed his eyes.

"I beg your pardon?" the clerk snapped at Maggie.

"I'm sorry, Alex," she said, ignoring the clerk. "I can't do this—not under these circumstances."

"You can't do this?" He looked angrier than she'd

ever seen him. "After all we've been through, *now* you can't do this?"

"I can't do it." She glanced at the clerk. "I'm awfully sorry to have wasted your time." Before Alex could stop her, she turned and raced from the room.

"Maggie!" He ran out after her.

She heard the clerk call, "Ten!" behind them.

Alex caught up with her outside. "Maggie!" He grabbed her arm and she whirled to face him.

"I'm sorry." Her eyes were fiery. "I can't do it. Sue me."

"Why are you deciding this now?"

"Because it suddenly hit me."

"What suddenly hit you?"

"That this is wrong. This isn't good for everyone involved, it's *horrible* for everyone involved. I can't subject Kate to living under a tense, loveless marriage. It didn't do me any good, and from what you tell me, it didn't do you any good, either. The fact that either one of us could contemplate doing that to a child is reprehensible."

"It's better than the alternative. The *inconsistency,* as you put it, of finding another nanny, of losing you."

"What about my leaving after three years? Did we really think that wouldn't matter?"

"We talked about you staying involved in her life."

"Even so, the breakup of what she would think of as her family would be devastating. Even if I lived next door."

"I still think that's better than losing you now."

Maggie shook her head. "I'm not sure it is."

"But things were fine. Kate's been happy. Nothing was going to change."

"Maybe that was the problem, too."

He shifted his weight and looked at her, exasperated. "*What* was the problem, too—that things weren't going to change?"

"Things did change, Alex. For me, not for you."

"What are you talking about?"

Tears filled her eyes and spilled onto her cheeks but she didn't care. "I have...feelings...for you, Alex." She sniffed. In for a penny, in for a pound. "I'm in love with you."

He looked shocked. That was the only word for it. His mouth dropped open and his glare burned her face. "In *love* with me?"

She felt mortification to her bones. "Which doesn't matter to you, I know, but it matters a heck of a lot to me. You probably think I'm weak, but I can't separate my feelings. And I cannot live that way."

The shock in his face relaxed a little and he closed his eyes briefly. He took a breath and said, "Maggie, I—I don't know what to say."

All her energy seemed to drain from her at once. "You don't have to say anything, just pat me on the shoulder and wish me luck."

"I do..." His voice trailed off.

Her heart pounded anew. "You do...?"

He didn't meet her eyes. "I do want you to stay."

"I've just told you why I can't." Senseless hope tugged at her heart as she looked at him.

There was a long silence.

Then Alex gave a single grave nod and said, "I'm sorry to see you go, but if that's your decision, I'll respect it."

"Kate, this is serious. We have to have a little chat." Alex stopped outside the door of the rec room and looked in. Kate was feeding the baby bird with an eye-dropper when Maggie reached for her hand and pulled her to one of the chairs.

"Have a seat," Maggie said, sitting across from her. "Beaky can finish in a moment."

"Do you think he's almost ready to fly?"

Maggie considered. "I think he is."

Kate's eyes were wide and unguarded. "I don't want him to fly away."

Maggie swallowed. This was going to be worse than she'd thought. "But that's the way life is. People, animals, everyone moves on. We all have different things we have to do, and different paths we have to take." She looked into Kate's puzzled expression and sighed. It wasn't going to be easy, but she had to just come out with it. "Do you remember when we talked about me staying here with you and your father?"

Kate ran a small finger across the bird's head. "Yup."

Maggie reached over and gently took her hand. "Things have changed a little bit," she said, leaning in toward Kate. Her voice broke and she cleared her throat.

Several yards away, Alex felt a constriction in his own throat. He clenched his jaw along with his fists.

"You're doing so well here, and getting ready to start first grade and all, that we've decided, your dad and I, that you might not need me so much after all. So I'm going back to England."

Kate's eyes widened. "*You're* leaving me?" She looked to the bird, then back at Maggie.

"I'm not leaving *you*," Maggie answered, realizing that she'd said these same words to Kate about her mother not so long ago. "You'll still have your dad and he'll take great care of you."

Kate's eyes filled with tears. "You can't leave! Does Daddy know you want to go? He won't let you go. He doesn't want you to go and I don't, either."

Maggie winced and Alex felt his own chest tighten like a vise. He leaned against the wall in the hall and put his head back, breathing deeply. This was for the best. Besides, Maggie wanted to go and he wasn't the sort to force her to stay, no matter how much he wanted her to.

Or, rather, needed her to. For Kate.

"You can't go!" Kate wailed in the other room. He moved to the doorway. "You can't leave me!" Tears flowed like rivers down her cheeks. "I want you to stay! Please stay, Maggie!" Her voice broke into sobs. "Everyone leaves me."

Alex's eyes burned and his mouth went dry. He had to do something. He didn't know what, but he had to do something to stop Kate's misery. And his own.

Without stopping to think what he'd do when he got in there, he entered the room. His eyes met Maggie's briefly, then he focused his attention on Kate. "Hey, there," he said softly. "What's all this crying about?"

"M-M-Maggie's l-l-l-leaving," Kate sobbed. Her lips trembled. "Sh-she wants to go back to England."

Alex looked at Maggie, whose eyes were glossy with unshed tears. "I know," he said. "You'll miss her a lot. She's going to have to come back for lots of visits." He looked at Maggie with raised eyebrows, and cocked his head in query.

"Of course, darling," Maggie said to Kate. "I'll come back. And you can come see me in England someday. You can meet my mum. She'd adore you and fill you up with biscuits and tea."

Kate turned to Alex with a sniffle. "We can't let Maggie go. "*You* have to stop her."

"Maggie's going because she has to." He thought quickly. Why *was* he letting her go?

What could he do to stop her?

"Her mother needs her," he finished saying.

"*We* need her."

"I know. But we'll be okay. Say, I have an idea." He looked around the room and saw a calendar on the wall. He went over and brought it back to Kate. "You have a Christmas vacation right around here." He pointed to a week in December. "I'll check my calendar and maybe we'll make plans to go to London. Maybe Maggie will show us around." He looked to Maggie.

She nodded mutely and swallowed, attempting a smile.

He looked back at Kate. "How does that sound to you?"

She sniffed. "Do you promise?"

He wrestled with that for a moment, trying to remember what he had scheduled for December. Then he looked back into Kate's eyes and nodded. "We'll figure it out. One way or another you'll go to England that week." To his relief, she didn't seem to notice he'd said "you'll go," but he knew Maggie did, and he felt her eyes burning on him even though he didn't face her. "Does that make you feel better?"

Kate wiped her eyes with the back of her hand. "No." When she put her hand down, Alex recognized a stoic reserve settling into Kate's expression. "So now you're going to hire *another* nanny, right?"

What could he say? He had to be honest, even though he knew she already knew the answer. "At least for a little while." He nodded.

Kate got off her chair and, without looking at Maggie, went back to where she'd been playing with her dolls.

Maggie watched with a slack jaw. "Kate? Don't you want to talk anymore? Do you have any questions?"

"No," Kate answered, without looking at her. "I don't have any questions." She returned her attention to her dolls.

Maggie looked at Alex. A thread of sadness pierced through him and he said to her, "I'm going back to work now. If you need any help with your final arrangements, let me know. I'll send Julia over." He stood for a moment, wishing he could think of something else to say.

"That's kind of you," Maggie replied stiffly. "But I'll be fine. Thanks. Kate, I'm going to get some things done." The child didn't answer. Maggie looked from her to Alex. "You both know where to find me if you need anything."

She turned and left, leaving Alex to wonder if he *would* know where to find her if he needed her.

Maggie had two more days before leaving the country and the first was filled with finalizing all the details of the past year of her life, including freezing her enrollment at the Institute until she could find out how to transfer credits when and if she was able to attend an associated school in the U.K.

She spent the next day interviewing prospective nannies. When Alex Harrison's secretary called the agencies, they all jumped to send the very best over for his consideration. He left it to Maggie to screen them.

It was a long, painful process. With every applicant who walked through the door, Maggie was reminded of what she'd almost had, and how very much she was going to lose.

"How much practical experience do you have with children?" Maggie asked one, a college student who was trying to decide whether to major in early childhood education or accounting.

"Practical experience?" she repeated vacantly. "You mean, like, have I ever been a nanny before? No, but don't tell the agency." She laughed and looked around her. "I think I could get used to *this*."

Maggie's heart dropped into her stomach. It hadn't occurred to her that people might take the job just for the quality of life in the mansion. Maybe she was naive, but she thought people would be interested in being a nanny because they were interested in helping children.

Another candidate was the oldest of seven children, had years of being a nursery school teaching assistant, and seemed like a good possibility until she dropped a bombshell: "As soon as I get over the morning sickness I should be ready to start work. Shouldn't be more than a month."

A distinct feeling of panic rose in Maggie's breast. She'd accepted the idea that she might not be able to find the *perfect* nanny for Kate but she had at least been certain she could find an adequate one. Now that was looking bleak.

The ninth applicant was a stern-faced middle-aged woman who had spent the last twenty-five years working as a nanny. Her references were impressive, but her bedside manner left something to be desired.

"You understand," Maggie told her, "that Kate has had some trouble with temper tantrums in the past. We need to be sure to find someone who can handle that properly."

"Oh, I can handle *that*," the woman assured her. "I won't stand for any nonsense at all. If she has a temper tantrum, she goes to bed without her supper. If it continues, there's always the belt."

"The belt?" Maggie took a deep breath and stood up, making an effort to keep her hands at her side instead of around the woman's throat. "Thank you, that will be all."

After she was gone, Maggie sank to her chair and cried. It felt as if her heart would explode. How on earth could she leave Kate to this fate? How could she live with herself knowing that Kate was living an ocean away without proper love and care?

But what choice did Maggie have? She couldn't stay, so she had to find someone.

She just *had* to.

After talking with seventeen possibilities, she ended up with two strong candidates. Both were older women, with years of experience working in households much like Alex's, and Maggie sensed great kindness in both. There had been no talk of missed suppers and both had been suitably horrified at the idea of corporal punishment.

Maggie didn't think either one was likely to give up on Kate if she had trouble with them at first. One was a former homemaker from Kansas City and the other was a British-trained nanny. Maggie wondered if Alex would pass over the British one simply because of her nationality.

Once burned, twice shy.

When the last candidate left, Maggie went into the kitchen to make a cup of tea. Her hand shook as she held the cup. Everywhere she looked, she saw something that made her feel weepy. Kate's drawings stuck on the refrigerator with magnets, a pair of saddle shoes carelessly strewn across the floor. Maggie had told Kate a hundred times to pick up her things, but now she smiled, seeing them.

But the smile faded quickly and Maggie's breath started to tremble. Was Kate going to be okay without her? Of course she would. Kate was going to have an excellent new nanny in either one of the candidates, someone who would be firm but kind, someone who would be with her long-term, who wouldn't have to leave and go thousands of miles away.

Maggie took a long breath and held it, trying to calm her pounding heart. She let the breath out and a sob caught in her throat. She never dreamed it would be this difficult.

A movement outside the window caught her eye. It was Alex, walking in the backyard, some distance away.

Alex.

Maggie's teeth sank into her lower lip. All of his problems were taken care of now. Maggie, the problem, would be out of his life. Within months he will have forgotten she'd ever been there. He didn't have to tether himself to her. He would have capable care for his daughter, so he didn't have to think of her. Maybe he would continue to be pestered by hungry women, but that wasn't anything he couldn't take care of. Obviously he must be very happy.

Maggie's eyes burned but remained dry. She was all cried out. But inside, something continued to wither. She couldn't look at him any longer, it hurt her heart.

With a deep, steadying breath she turned and left the room.

Alex walked alone in the backyard. The heat was pounding, and he loosened his tie and unbuttoned the top few buttons of his shirt.

He couldn't believe Maggie was leaving. He thought she took her commitments more seriously than that. They'd drawn up their concerns, each one of them, and incorporated them into a prenuptial agreement. They were supposed to be married.

Instead she was leaving.

His jaw tightened. After he'd admitted that he wanted her to stay, she was leaving anyway. How much more could he have done? Did she want him to beg? Well, he wasn't going to do that. Alex Harrison was not used to getting down on his knees, and he wasn't going to start now.

Didn't Maggie even care about leaving Kate? Maybe not. She knew Kate didn't want her to leave, either, but she was going anyhow.

He stopped. The pink playhouse was in front of him. A trio of dolls sat by an upside-down box, with three plastic cups on top of it. Kate had been having a tea party with her dolls by Her House. There was a strange twinge in his chest. He sat down next to the dolls in the shade of the elm tree and looked at them. The painted smiles were relentless, little arms all open wide. They were built that way on purpose, easy to hug. Sort of like a child, Alex thought despite himself. He pictured Kate playing here with the dolls, and running in and out of the little house. He'd seen her do it but only for a moment. Then he'd had to go back in for a meeting.

Maggie would have hated that.

Alex hated it. Kate wasn't going to be little forever. Already memories of her babyhood drifted away like long-ago ghosts, like someone he would never see again. If he didn't take more care then this Kate, this innocent, forgiving, loving, bright-eyed child, would be replaced by someone else. He picked a leaf off a gnarled root beside him. Who knew how much joy would be in the eyes of the next Kate? Especially if the people who loved her had to leave, or were so afraid to let their love show that they kept it all bundled inside.

An image of his own father came to mind and for the first time in his memory he didn't feel sick at the thought. His father was dead and gone. Alex wasn't him. Alex wasn't even like him. He had control over his actions, just as Maggie had said.

Somehow he'd never fully believed that before.

He tore the leaf in half. Afraid. He was afraid. He'd never gone so far as to admit that before. He tore the leaf again. He was afraid that if he gave the love he felt away, there would be nothing left.

Maggie would have told him that was stupid.

He tossed the pieces of leaf to the ground and stood up. Without even bothering to dust the dirt off his pants he set off for the house, to find Kate. He had to get to her fast. Yes, Kate had said she hated him. Maybe she even meant it. But even if she did, maybe—just maybe—he could *change* that. Maybe it wasn't too late for her to love him. He had to start being her father, for real, before it was too late. There was no more reason to play it safe, because safe wasn't so safe after all. It had cost him years already. He'd lost time with Kate that he could never make up. He had to stop the cycle.

He had nothing left to lose.

Maggie had four hours before it was time to leave. She'd said her goodbyes to everyone and arranged for an old friend to pick her up at Heathrow Airport in

London. Now she had only to go to her room and double-check that she'd packed everything.

She didn't want to have to call once she was gone, to have anything shipped to her.

Though her footsteps echoed through the wide hallway as she made her way to the stairs, she heard something else. She stopped, held her breath and listened closely. There it was again. Something here didn't make sense. Kate didn't normally talk to herself.

Maggie froze. There was a low vibration, the sound of a male voice. Then Kate exploded into giggles.

Maggie followed the laughter up the stairs to Kate's room. When she stopped at the door she couldn't believe what she saw. Alex sat Indian-style on the floor in front of the Candyland game board. Kate knelt on the other side of it, merrily hopping her red playing piece along the course to the Queen Frostine square right near the end.

"I'm gonna win!" Kate squealed with delight.

"Two out of three wins," Alex replied with a smile. "You've only won one so far."

"I'm almost to the end," she said in a singsongy voice.

"But no one has picked the candy cane card yet," he said, then drew a card. "Aw!" He pretended to clutch at his chest and fall to the floor. The candy cane card slipped out of his hand.

Kate laughed with near-hysterical glee. "You got it! You got it!"

"Three games out of five," Alex said.

"Yippee!"

"And the loser has to take the winner out for an ice cream."

"But I can't drive." Kate frowned. "What if I lose?"

"Then I'll drive," Alex told her with a reassuring smile. "But I have a feeling you won't need to worry about that. You're cleaning up at this game."

Maggie drew back from the doorway and leaned against the wall. Finally Alex and Kate were connecting. It's what Maggie had been watching for during the past five months. She smiled faintly. Kate had looked so happy. So *open.* She didn't have a shred of curiosity about where her father had been before. He was in front of her now, reaching out to her, and she was accepting with the blind trust that only a child has.

Maybe everything *was* going to be all right for them.

Maggie swallowed hard over the lump in her throat and went down the hall to her bedroom. Something must have accounted for the change. Was it vain of her to think she may have had something to do with it? That, after all they had been through and as painful as the push and pull had been, she may have ultimately been able to help?

It didn't matter. Something had changed and she was glad to see it. She didn't *feel* glad, but she was. This was the very thing she'd set out to accomplish. Maybe one game didn't make a relationship, but certainly Kate was on the road to having a healthy relationship with Alex. He in turn would experience the pleasure and gratification that can only come with a child's love and trust. She *was* happy for them.

So why did she want so badly to cry?

Maggie rounded the corner into her bedroom and flopped down onto the bed. A headache pounded its way through her brain. She knew what was wrong. She knew exactly why she couldn't share in the joy of Alex and Kate's progress.

Because of that childish voice that cried inside her head, *They didn't need me after all.*

Chapter Ten

It was time to go.

Maggie was in the hall surrounded by suitcases. She was picking up the phone to call a cab when Alex appeared.

"So you're going."

She looked at him, surprised. "Of course."

He shook his head impatiently. "I meant *now*. You're going *now?*"

She eyed him evenly. "Yes. I was about to call a cab." She waited for his response.

"You don't have to do that," he began.

Senseless hope stirred.

"Mike can drive you," he finished saying.

Hope rolled over and died. "That's very generous but a cab will be just fine." She waited a moment. "Thanks anyway."

"Did Kate get a chance to say goodbye?"

The fact that he could ask such a question showed that she had misjudged him as much as he had misjudged her. "Of course. Mrs. McGregor has taken her to a movie. I thought it was best to avoid a difficult emotional scene when I left."

"Kate will be all right." Inside he wondered.

"I meant me."

"Ah." Somehow he had trouble believing that. After all, she was leaving. She had made that choice.

They stood facing each other, neither speaking.

Finally Maggie said, "Well, goodbye." She extended her hand. "It's been…" Her voice trailed off.

"It's been a pleasure," he finished, in a maddeningly businesslike voice. He took her hand in his.

She met his eyes.

He dropped her hand.

"Why are you still angry at me?" Maggie heard herself asking. "Mrs. McGregor is a wonderful nanny. Everything will be fine for you. I don't understand why *you're* being so cold."

His face was impassive. "I'm sorry you feel that way."

She clenched her teeth. "Forget it." She picked up the telephone receiver.

He didn't stop her.

She dialed the cab company and arranged to have one take her to the airport. When she hung up, Alex was still standing there.

"Is there anything else I can do for you?" he asked. When she didn't answer at first, he said, "Do you need help carrying these bags out?"

"No, thanks." She gestured weakly. "I only have the two."

He let out a long breath. "Maggie, there's really something I need to say to you."

She eyed him warily. "Yes?"

"I—" He stopped. The clock ticked loudly through the hall. Somewhere outside a dog barked.

"You what, Alex?"

"I..." He looked down at the floor, then around at all the walls, then at the door behind her, before meeting her eyes.

Her stomach constricted. She faced him, willing herself not to fill the silence with inane babble. Finally he spoke.

"I...I just want you to know you'll always be welcome back here."

The cab horn blasted outside.

What did that mean? That she was always welcome to reapply for the job or that she was welcome back to be with him? She wasn't going to ask, because she wasn't prepared to hear either answer. Not that it mattered. Either way he wasn't saying that he loved her and would go to any length to keep her with him.

It was all she could do to find her voice. "I have to go." She picked up her suitcases and pushed through the door. Every step she took, she could feel his eyes on her as she walked to the waiting car.

Alex watched her go with one hand on the doorknob and felt his chest constrict with every step she took. She was going. The doorknob felt icy under his touch. Maggie was leaving and he felt as if something in him was dying. They both always knew she would go someday, if not this month then in three more months. They always knew she would be leaving the area as soon as the term of their marriage was up. So why did he feel so miserable now? She was the nanny, that was all.

Why this strange feeling of shock and loss to him?

The saying was "all's well that ends well," and all

of his problems were solved. The new nanny seemed perfect, as nannies went. A regular Mary Poppins.

But not a Maggie Weller.

Maggie couldn't be replaced. Had he really thought she could be? Had he really even wanted to replace her? He knew the answer—he'd known it all along. No one else could hold a candle to her.

The cab drew out of the driveway and Alex watched the headlights bounce along the trees as it left. *Stop,* he thought. *Give me some time to think.* His grasp on the doorknob tightened. Part of him wanted to run after her, to grab her and beg her to stay. But the other part of him wouldn't let him—wouldn't move—because... why? Because he was scared she might leave him someday?

He swallowed and tightened his grip until his fingers cramped. He was ready to let the best thing that had ever happened to him slip away because he was *scared* she might leave someday? Would he be any worse off then than he was now?

Yes. He let go of the knob. The closer he got to Maggie, the more difficult it would have been to see her go. This was the right thing to do. He would be a fool to trust another woman, after the hell he'd been through with his first wife. Marriage didn't work for him. Maybe he just wasn't the right type. He would be a fool to think that he had something to offer Maggie after the effort he'd made to eliminate all marital emotions.

But then, she had been the one to convince him that he had something to offer Kate, and she'd been right. Maybe he had something to offer her, too. There might be some way to convince her of that. Maybe this crushing feeling in his chest would amount to something good, if he let it.

He had to do something to change this horrible feeling. He had to get Maggie back into his life and keep her there. It was a hell of a chance to take, but he had to do it. He had to have Maggie. No matter what the risk.

For the first time in years he was willing to take that chance.

He couldn't let her go!

He wanted her. He wanted her in his bed every night and in the kitchen having coffee with him every morning. He wanted to travel with her, to go to openings and exhibits and business dinners with her, he wanted to build more things with her. He wanted to build a life with her.

He had to get her!

He dashed to the kitchen, looking for his keys. *Please get stuck in traffic,* he prayed silently, thinking of the cab. *Slow down. Make her miss the flight.* His search for the keys grew frantic. They weren't in the usual place by the door and he stood for interminable minutes trying to concentrate on where he had been, where he might have left them.

The bedroom. He took the stairs two at a time and threw the door open. In three strides he was across the room. He opened the top dresser drawer.

Empty. *Damn* it.

He noticed his pants lying across the bed and picked them up. They jingled. He grabbed the keys, tearing the pocket in his haste, and ran down to the car.

It wouldn't start.

Be calm, he told himself. *This is just some sort of karmic revenge for taking so long to realize what I have to do*. He took a breath. The Fate he had always heard of wouldn't allow him to be stranded in his garage, trying to start his car while the woman he loved boarded a jet. He tried the ignition again.

It started.

The woman he loved? Had he really thought those words? Yes. His heart pounded and a new urgency took over. Yes, he loved her. He loved her!

He jerked the Jaguar into reverse and squealed out of the garage, knocking over two trash cans in the process. He didn't care. All he knew was that he had to stop her and the feeling grew stronger with each passing minute.

He drove, too fast, through the night. Several big raindrops splashed on his windshield and before long, the sky was pouring and the road was slick. The highway in front of him was a sea of flaring red brake lights. He tried not to look at the digital clock on his dashboard, ticking the minutes away at an alarming rate.

By the time he got to the airport, the rain was coming down so hard he could barely see three feet in front of him. Windshield wipers slapped ineffectively at the deluge as he searched the sea of cabs for the one that had taken her away.

Then, like an angel, he spotted her.

A soggy angel, but an angel nevertheless. She was standing by the cab as the driver took her bags out of the trunk. Alex pulled up as close as he could get to them, which was three cars back. He threw the car out of gear, pulled up the emergency brake and pushed open the door.

Rain smacked him in the face. "Maggie!" he yelled.

She straightened, then looked around.

"Maggie! Here!" he called again, trying to make his

way through the maze of cars, cabs and airport limousines.

This time she saw him and looked quickly away.

"You can't leave," he called, closer now.

"I *am* leaving," she called back.

"But I need you to stay," he returned. Car horns began blasting behind him. His car would either get totaled or towed, but he didn't care. "I want you to stay, please."

"Stay, Maggie," a snarly voice called from behind him. "So he'll get his damned car out of the way."

Alex ignored it. He ran to her and stopped, inches away, breathless and desperate. "I want *you,*" he said. "All of you." He grabbed her hand and held it tightly in his. "Not just Maggie the nanny."

"You want more." She yanked her arm free. "You've made that clear on more than one occasion. My answer is *no.*"

"Why? Because you don't think this marriage could work? Or because you don't want it to work?"

Tears brimmed in her eyes. "Why are you tormenting me with this? I've told you I cannot separate the physical from the emotional. I can't just add sex to our arrangement and be happy—"

"Neither can I."

"I know men can sleep with multiple women and never care one iota for any but for you to talk about our marriage *working*— What did you say?"

He put his hands on her damp shoulders and looked deeply into her eyes. "I said neither can I." He laughed once and shrugged. "You probably won't believe this, but I love you, Maggie Weller." He let go of her shoulders and jerked his thumb toward the car he had just left. "I want to take you home and spend the rest of my life proving it."

Though it was hard to tell in the rain, he thought he saw tears spill down Maggie's cheeks, mixing with rain-drops. Her mouth opened, then shut. She closed her eyes tightly then looked back at him. "I can't believe this."

"You'd better believe it." He was fired up now. He paced on the street in front of her. "You've ruined my life, such as it was. Work isn't an escape anymore. The house is too damn big and that nanny, wonderful as she is, just irks the hell out of me." Someone leaned on a car horn and Alex had to yell to be heard over the noise. "Everything makes me think of you, makes me want you more."

She drew a shuddering breath but didn't speak.

"There's more," Alex said. "I can't pretend that Kate will be okay without me anymore, I have to take a chance on being there for her." He smiled. "I'm committed to that."

Maggie's smile was a bit melancholy. "Good. Then you're seeing what I've said all along. All Kate really needs is you, whether you're perfect or not."

"That's not entirely true. Yes, you were right when you said that she needs me. I can see that now. And I can see that I have a lot to offer her."

"That's what I said."

He put a finger to her lips. "But I was right, too, Maggie. I'm *not* enough. She needs you, too. Not only because she loves you and there would be a terrible void if you left, but as she grows up she'll need your advice on the changes in her body, and on dating, and on dealing with a difficult man like her father from time to time.''

"Dealing with you from time to time?'' Maggie asked with a smile and a sniff.

He wiped tears and raindrops from her cheek. "No, difficult from time to time.'' He rested his wrist on her shoulder and continued to gently caress her cheek.

"Are you sure this isn't all because you don't want to go through the nanny process again?''

"You know we hired a perfect nanny yesterday. I'm letting her go tomorrow. Whether you come back with me or not.'' He cupped her face in his hands and gave her a long, hard kiss. "Please come back with me.''

She pulled back and searched his face. "Am I an idiot to believe this?''

"Maggie, I've been an idiot so long, I can't even begin to distinguish lines. All I know is if you listen to your heart that's the only way you're ever going to know the truth.'' He shook his head. "I can't even believe I'm saying something so corny, but it's true.'' He took her hand and held it against his pounding heart. "I've got to believe this. Do you?''

She lifted his hand to her lips and held it there for a long silent moment. "I do.''

"Say it again.''

She met his eyes. "I do.''

"Then you've got to tell me something, and tell me the truth. Do you love me?''

Hot tears burned in her eyes as she faced him, faced her feelings for him. She knew what they were, what they had been all along. Love. For all his faults and weaknesses and strengths and virtues, she loved him. "I told you I did before,'' she said. "I meant it.''

"Are you sure you love me, Maggie?'' he asked

again softly, more tentatively.

"I do." She threw her arms around him and fell into his embrace. "Oh, I do."

At eleven o'clock the next morning they were driving across the Chesapeake Bay Bridge.

"Why won't you tell me where we're going?" Maggie asked with a laugh.

"You'll see," he said cryptically. "I've pretty much bungled everything else that's happened in this relationship so far. I want today to be a new start for us." He looked heavenward and Maggie thought she detected a silent prayer.

"There's still the matter of the INS board hearing," she reminded him.

"If the INS board doesn't believe us now, they're going to have to send me back to England with you."

She smiled at the idea of taking him to meet her mother, to visit the village that had been her home for so long.

Several quiet minutes passed companionably.

"Oh, I nearly forgot." She reached down and rummaged through her purse. "A registered letter came while we were picking up our things at the house. It's for you." She looked at the return address. "From Stan Wilkins, Esquire. Isn't that your lawyer?"

"Put it away," Alex said. "I don't want any more bad news from Stan right now."

"Maybe it's not bad news."

"He's been calling since right after the Callam Gash debacle. It's bad news."

"Okay. If you say so." Maggie shrugged and put the envelope back into her purse.

They drove into a small eastern seaboard town called Hanson. The streets were lined with tall oak trees, and every house looked like a variation on the gingerbread theme. Alex pulled the car up in front of the last one on Main Street. It was enormous, with tall round columns and magnolia trees lining a wraparound porch. The small yard was partitioned by a black wrought-iron fence. The gate had a brass plaque that read R.V. Shippett, Justice of the Peace.

Still in the car, Maggie turned watery eyes to Alex. "You've got to be joking," she said.

He shook his head, taking the keys out of the ignition. "Not a chance."

"But this is just like an old movie."

"No, no. In the movies something usually goes wrong. Nothing, but *nothing,* is going to go wrong with this." He got out of the car and went around to open her door.

"What if he's not at home?" she asked as she stepped onto the sidewalk.

"He's home. I called first."

She raised an eyebrow. "Ah, so this isn't as spontaneous as it first seemed."

Alex held out a hand and tipped it from side to side. "I called from a pay phone when we stopped for drinks. Just to be sure."

"You just happened to have the number?"

"Yeah, I keep it in an 'if all else fails take her to the judge' file."

"Alex!"

"Okay, I had the operator connect me to the town hall and they gave me his number."

"No wonder you took so long." She thought of the long minutes she'd spent in the car thinking he was on business calls that were too important to let lie for a few hours. Thank goodness she hadn't said anything at the time.

"Are you ready to become Mrs. Harrison once and for all?"

"I'm ready." She inhaled deeply. Someone in the neighborhood was having a cookout and she reveled in the smoky scent on the hot summer breeze. All around were sounds of children playing and people laughing. This was heaven.

He put his hand on the gate but didn't open it. "You realize this means that contract is going in the trash as soon as we get home."

"I do."

"And you realize also that all this business about no sex, that's history, too."

"I do."

"And you know that I'm never letting you go, not in three years or thirty."

She nodded with a smile. "I do."

He opened the gate and held out his arm. "Good. Then I think we're ready."

She hooked her arm through his and they went to the front door. He pushed the button and the doorbell chimed inside. Presently it was opened by a small gray-haired woman wearing wire-rimmed glasses and an apron over a flower print dress.

"Mr. Harrison?" she asked.

"Yes. This is my fiancée, Maggie Weller."

The woman gave her a kind smile. "Hello, dear, we've been expecting you. I'm Mrs. Shippett. Please come this way."

They followed her into a large drawing room with high ceilings and a Victorian settee and chairs. There was a silver tea service on an end table.

"Would you like some tea?" Mrs. Shippett asked.

"Thank you," Maggie said.

Alex shook his head.

Mrs. Shippett poured steaming tea into a delicate china cup and held it out to Maggie. "Cream or lemon?"

"I take it plain, thanks."

Mrs. Shippett set the teapot down and said, "If you'll excuse me, I'll just let my husband know that you're ready."

She disappeared into another room and Maggie turned to Alex. "These are actors you've hired, right?"

He splayed his arms. "No, I swear it. This is for real. You'd better know that going into it."

She took a sip of the steaming tea and set it down. "And you'd better know I plan on holding you to it."

The back door opened and an old man who looked like one of Santa's elves came doddering out. Like his wife, he wore glasses but his were dark and horn-rimmed. His back was slightly hunched, but his face was youthful in its merry countenance. "I'm sorry to keep you folks waiting. I'm Judge Shippett, how do you do?"

Alex shook his hand. "Alex Harrison. How do you do, sir. This is my fiancée, Maggie Weller."

"How do you do, Miss Weller?" The man took Maggie's hand and he said with a wink. "Not *Miss* for long, eh?" He looked behind them. "Stella, are you going to play the piano for these nice folks?"

"Certainly," Mrs. Shippett said behind them. "As soon as I give Ms. Weller her flowers." She approached Maggie, followed by a girl in a white apron, and held out a bouquet of miniature roses and baby's breath as well as several stalks of what Maggie recognized as rosemary.

"It's good luck," Mrs. Shippett said.

"Rosemary for remembrance," Maggie mused to herself.

"What's that?" Alex said next to her.

She smiled into his eyes. "It's old herbal lore." She looked back at the flowers. "Rosemary signifies remembrance."

Mrs. Shippett went to the piano and sat down. A moment later the familiar wedding march boomed around them.

When the music ended, Judge Shippett began. "Dearly beloved, we are gathered here today to celebrate the marriage of this man and this woman in the presence of God and these witnesses." He beamed at his wife and at the girl in the apron. "Marriage is an honorable institution, not to be entered into lightly but thoughtfully and reverently." He stopped and beamed at them both. "And I must say I've never seen two people who looked more in love with each other."

Maggie and Alex glanced at each other and laughed.

Judge Shippett's service continued. "Margaret, do you take this man to be your lawfully wedded husband, to love, honor and cherish all the days of your life? Will you have him in sickness and in health, for richer and for poorer, and forsaking all others keep thee only unto him for as long as you both shall live?"

Maggie looked at Alex and this time her heart was not fluttering but rather beating steadily with a quiet certainty. "I will."

Judge Shippett looked pleased. "Good, good. Now Alexander, do you take this woman to be your lawfully wedded wife, to love, honor and cherish all the days of your life? Will you have her in sickness and in health, for richer and for poorer, and forsaking all others keep thee only unto her for as long as you both shall live?"

Alex didn't hesitate this time. "I will."

"Do you have rings?"

Alex handed him Maggie's ring. "We haven't had time to get another one."

"Ah, ah, ah." Maggie rummaged and pulled a gold ring out of her purse. "I got this before…for the courthouse. I'd been carrying it around, waiting for an opportunity to return it, but I forgot. Until now." She presented it to the judge.

He handed Maggie's ring to Alex and said, "Repeat after me. With this ring, I thee wed."

Alex slid the ring onto her finger and said, looking into her eyes, "With this ring, I thee wed." His voice was thick with emotion.

Judge Shippett handed Maggie the other ring. "Repeat after me. With this ring, I thee wed."

"With this ring, I thee wed." *If it fits it's all real. Oh, please let it fit, let it fit.* It slid easily onto his finger.

They both smiled.

Judge Shippett concluded. "What the Lord and this state have joined together, let no man tear asunder." He looked at Alex. "You may now kiss your bride."

Alex bent down, but because of their audience it was a brief kiss, leaving both wanting more. Mrs. Shippett burst into song again on the piano and Alex and Maggie both laughed.

"Well, finally it's all gone right," Maggie said. "This was the best wedding yet."

Alex smiled, and was about to comment when he

remembered Stan Wilkins's letter. "Let me see that letter," he said to Maggie thoughtfully.

"Now?"

He nodded. "I just had a thought..."

She got the letter out and watched while he opened it. When he'd finished reading, he folded it back up and put it into his pocket, a wide grin on his face.

"What is it?" Maggie said. "Has he found a loophole to get you out of this marriage?"

"Hardly. You might say we're doubly married."

"What do you mean?"

"Callam Gash. He renewed his license last week. We were legally married the first time."

Maggie reached up and touched his smile. "But we weren't *really* married until right now."

A loud *pop* came from the corner and Maggie saw Judge Shippett pouring glasses of bubbly. He carried two of them over and handed one to each of them.

"It's sparkling cider," the judge said in a low voice. "She," he indicated his wife, "won't let me keep anything else in the house." He winked.

Maggie laughed. "It's perfect."

"Happy?" Alex asked Maggie.

"Delirious."

"Do you remember the toast I proposed that day in the wine cellar?"

She thought for a moment, then nodded. "Yes, you said 'to Maggie's wedding.'"

He looked around at the lovely drawing room, the small bouquet in her hand and at the beaming older couple who had gone through it with them. "I think we did it right." He raised his glass to her. "To Maggie's wedding."

"To *our* marriage," she said, correcting him.

He smiled and nodded slightly. "Forever."

Their gazes lingered; they touched their glasses and drank to a bright future.

* * * * *

Share in the joy of yuletide romance with brand-new
stories by two of the genre's most beloved writers

DIANA PALMER

and

JOAN JOHNSTON

in

LONE STAR CHRISTMAS

Diana Palmer and Joan Johnston share their favorite
Christmas anecdotes and personal stories in this
special hardbound edition.

Diana Palmer delivers an irresistible spin-off of her
LONG, TALL TEXANS series and Joan Johnston crafts an
unforgettable new chapter to **HAWK'S WAY** in this wonderful
keepsake edition celebrating the holiday season. So
perfect for gift giving, you'll want one for yourself...and
one to give to a special friend!

Available in November at your favorite retail outlet!

Only from

V *Silhouette*®

Take 4 bestselling love stories FREE

Plus get a FREE surprise gift!

Special Limited-time Offer

Mail to Silhouette Reader Service™

3010 Walden Avenue
P.O. Box 1867
Buffalo, N.Y. 14240-1867

YES! Please send me 4 free Silhouette Romance™ novels and my free surprise gift. Then send me 6 brand-new novels every month, which I will receive months before they appear in bookstores. Bill me at the low price of $2.67 each plus 25¢ delivery and applicable sales tax, if any.* That's the complete price and a savings of over 10% off the cover prices—quite a bargain! I understand that accepting the books and gift places me under no obligation ever to buy any books. I can always return a shipment and cancel at any time. Even if I never buy another book from Silhouette, the 4 free books and the surprise gift are mine to keep forever.

215 BPA A3UT

Name	(PLEASE PRINT)	
Address	Apt. No.	
City	State	Zip

This offer is limited to one order per household and not valid to present Silhouette Romance™ subscribers. *Terms and prices are subject to change without notice. Sales tax applicable in N.Y.

USROM-696

©1990 Harlequin Enterprises Limited

Bestselling author

JOAN JOHNSTON

continues her wildly popular miniseries with an
all-new, longer-length novel

The Virgin Groom

HAWK'S WAY

One minute, Mac Macready was a living legend in
Texas—every kid's idol, every man's envy, every
woman's fantasy. The next, his fiancée dumped him,
his career was hanging in the balance and his future
was looking mighty uncertain. Then there was the
matter of his scandalous secret, which didn't stand a
chance of staying a secret. So would he succumb to
Jewel Whitelaw's shocking proposal—or take cold
showers for the rest of the long, hot summer...?

Available August 1997
wherever Silhouette books are sold.

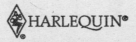

Silhouette ROMANCE™

COMING NEXT MONTH

#1240 BABY BUSINESS—Laura Anthony

Bundles of Joy

Caring for infants was business as usual to lovely pediatrician Tobie Avery, but when millionaire bachelor Clay Barton asked for her help, Tobie wondered if the baby's rugged uncle would consider her for a more permanent position—as his wife!

#1241 WYATT'S MOST WANTED WIFE—Sandra Steffen

Bachelor Gulch

Lisa Markman came to Jasper Gulch looking for a husband and a new life. But Sheriff Wyatt McCully, a man with a reputation as sterling as his badge, *wasn't* the man for her, no matter how sexy or intriguing he was! Especially if the handsome lawman found out about the past she was fleeing....

#1242 MARRY IN HASTE—Moyra Tarling

Jade had never forgotten the man who had pledged her his heart, and then torn it away. Now devastatingly handsome Evan Mathieson had returned, and was asking once again for her hand in marriage. But could Jade trust their love a second time, when she harbored a terrible secret that touched them both?

#1243 HUSBAND IN RED—Cara Colter

Sadie McGee was back home to care for her family. Romance was *not* in her plans. But Michael O'Bryan, the town's golden boy, had never forgotten the sexy girl from the wrong side of the tracks—and would win her back no matter what....

#1244 THE RAINBOW BRIDE—Elizabeth Sites

A Western wedding? Pretty librarian Iris Merlin came to the old town of Felicity looking for answers to her family's scandalous past, not love! But rugged Adam Freemont soon captured her passion, and had Iris dreaming of becoming the gorgeous man's wife.

**#1245 MARRIAGE IS JUST THE BEGINNING—
       Betty Jane Sanders**

To keep his little girl, single father Grant Parker would gladly marry the lovely Sharon O'Riley—in name only. After all, Sharon had known little Cassie since birth, and treated her as her own. But this caring, warm beauty also had other charms, and Grant soon suspected that marriage to Sharon was just the beginning....

Wanted: Brides! This small South Dakota town needs women of marriageable age. And *Silhouette Romance* invites you to visit the handsome, extremely eligible men of:

a new miniseries by
Sandra Steffen

♥ The local veterinarian finds himself falling for his feisty receptionist—the one woman in town *not* interested in finding herself a husband.

LUKE'S WOULD-BE BRIDE
(June '97)

♥ This sheriff's got a reputation for being the good guy, yet a certain single gal has him wanting to prove just what a wolf in sheep's clothing he really is.

WYATT'S MOST WANTED WIFE
(August '97)

♥ A rugged rancher proposes a marriage of convenience to a dowdy diner waitress, but just wait till his ugly-duckling bride turns into a swan.

CLAYTON'S MADE-OVER MRS.
(October '97)

Don't miss any of these wonderful love stories, available only from

Silhouette ROMANCE™